Maple Glaze and Murder

Holly Holmes Culinary Mystery - book 9

K.E. O'Connor

K.E. O'Connor Books

While every precaution has been taken in the preparation of this book, the publisher assumes no responsibility for errors or omissions, or for damages resulting from the use of the information contained herein.

All rights reserved.

No portion of this book may be reproduced in any form without written permission from the publisher or author, except as permitted by U.S. copyright law.

MAPLE GLAZE AND MURDER – LARGE PRINT EDITION

ISBN: 978-1-918248-15-9

Written by K.E. O'Connor

Chapter 1

I adjusted the lace around my neckline and smoothed the pale fabric of my full-length silk dress. I took a deep breath, and it came out shaky.

I stared at myself in the mirror in my bed-room. I almost didn't recognize the woman staring back at me. My dark hair was shining and had a slight wave to it, and my make-up had been done by an expert, so my eyes looked huge and my mouth glossy. I was more used to flour smeared on my cheek and chocolate on my apron.

Meatball, my beloved corgi cross, sat on my bed, watching my every move. Beside him sat Saffron, my gran's dog. They wore fetching bow ties, Meatball's in black and Saffron's in red, and were ready for the wedding to begin.

I glanced at the large bouquet of cream and yellow flowers waiting for me. "What do you think, pooches? Are we ready to go?"

Saffron gave a little whine, and Meatball wagged his tail.

"This is an important day. Everything needs to go right. We can't let the families down."

Meatball wagged his tail again, and Saffron lifted one paw.

"And it's a big day for both of you. Be on your best behavior when you walk along that aisle. You wouldn't have been picked to be a groomsman or a doggie bridesmaid if I didn't think you could be relied on."

I had no worries about Meatball behaving. He'd be an angel, unless he sniffed out a tasty piece of sausage hidden in someone's pocket. But Saffron was another matter. She could be a stubborn lady when she wanted to be and wasn't a fan of crowds. And there'd be plenty of people at the wedding this afternoon.

I peeked out the window and smiled. It was perfect wedding weather. Fluffy white clouds drifted across a bright blue sky. There was barely any wind, but it wasn't too warm, so I wouldn't sweat in my elegant dress.

The bedroom door behind me burst open, and Princess Alice Audley raced through. She grabbed my hands. "Holly, you look so pretty. Even prettier than me, and I didn't think that was possible." She twirled me, and I laughed.

Alice looked stunning in a green silk gown. Her blonde curls were piled loosely on her head, and a sparkling tiara nestled among them.

"I can't believe this is happening. I'm so excited," she said.

"Me too. But I'm nervous. All those people are waiting in the castle."

"Don't worry about them. They'll only be thinking good thoughts about you when they see you in that dress," Alice said. "But you need to hurry. You can't be late today."

"I'm ready to go," I said. "Did you see Gran when you came in?"

Alice nodded. "She looks twice as nervous as you. Grab your flowers, let's get a move on."

I caught hold of my bouquet, then hurried out of the bedroom, Meatball and Saffron following me. I entered the lounge to find Gran standing by the window staring out of it.

"Alice, you take the dogs outside and give them a run before we head to the castle. Make sure they burn off any excess energy so they behave themselves."

"I'm on it. Come on, fluff balls." Alice took the dogs out and shut the door behind her.

I walked over to Gran and touched her shoulder. "You make a beautiful bride."

She turned, and I sucked in a breath as I saw tears in her eyes. "I'm not sure I can go through with this. What am I thinking, getting married at my age?"

"Gran! You can get married at any age. You and Ray are perfect for each other."

"Oh, I love the man, probably too much. But all this fuss. I should have had a ceremony in the local village hall and then a couple of drinks in the pub."

"Alice and Rupert wouldn't want you getting married anywhere else. This venue is perfect, and it's our home. It's only right you get married here. And the ceremony room looks stunning."

"It's too grand for me. I didn't grow up posh, and I shouldn't pretend now. I'm not sure I should have all of this."

"You deserve it." My gran had been through rough times, many of them partly her fault, after she stole from rich men. It was a revenge tactic after she got cheated out of her life savings by a lothario. But she'd served her time and was a reformed character, and she'd met the love of her life when she'd moved to Audley St. Mary. Ray was a kind, sweet man, and he was besotted with Gran, just as he should be.

Gran turned and looked out the window again. "It was generous of the Audleys to let me have the castle rooms for my wedding."

"It's their wedding gift to you and Ray. Ray's worked at Audley Castle for years, so they want to do right by him. And they like having you here, too."

"And all the flowers came from the gardens, and the catering is being done by Chef Heston ..."

"Don't forget, I made your wedding cake."

"And it'll be delicious." Gran smiled at me. "Oh, Holly! You look lovely in that dress. I suppose I shouldn't let everyone down by pulling out so late in the day."

"You love Ray, and he loves you. That's all that matters. Forget about everyone else and the swanky surroundings, just focus on that. That's what's important about today."

"What if ..." She went to chew on her nail.

I stopped her spoiling her manicure by catching hold of her hand. "Is something else worrying you?"

Gran's gaze dropped to the floor. "I don't want to let Ray down."

"Why would you do that?"

"He knows about my past. I'm far from per-fect."

"None of us are perfect. But you're different now. And you've got Ray, Saffron, and me to keep you on the straight and narrow if you ever need a nudge in the right direction. The only way you'll let Ray down is if you don't get a wiggle on and get married to him."

"We should have gone to Las Vegas. We could have hopped on a plane, met an Elvis impersonator, and been done with it." She waved a hand at her fitted cream dress with its beautiful sparkling diamantes around the hem.

"And then you'd have missed seeing most of your friends and family who want to congratulate you. Plus, Saffron and Meatball would have hated to travel such a long way, and you wouldn't want them missing out. Did you see their bow ties?"

"I did. They're cute. And, no, I don't want them missing out. They're a part of our family."

"You deserve to be pampered. Enjoy the day."

She took a deep breath and squeezed my hand. "You're right. It's just my nerves."

"Of course. Now, is there anything you need before we leave?"

Gran puffed out a breath. "Remind me how to breathe again."

I carefully kissed her cheek, making sure not to disturb the light covering of pretty make-up on her face. I couldn't be more delighted that she was marrying Ray. They made each other so happy.

I picked up her bouquet and handed it to her. "It's time to go."

She nodded. "And once this is over, you can start thinking about getting married to Rupert. He's a catch. My granddaughter, not only is she royal, she's also marrying a lord!"

I smiled, still a little starry eyed over the fact Lord Rupert Audley had proposed to me. And I'd turned him down! Well, it had been a shock proposal. We'd barely been on a real date, and there he was, on his knee asking me to be with him forever.

But we'd been seriously dating for several months, and everything had been going amazingly well. And Rupert really wanted to get married. Secretly, so did I, but I refused to be rushed into such a huge decision. Change was scary, and I was a bit of a coward when it came to big upheaval. I liked a quiet, simple life, but it wouldn't be so simple once I married into the Audley family.

"One wedding at a time, Gran," I said.

"She's in here! This way, ladies."

I turned at the sound of an unfamiliar voice approaching the front door. It was pushed open, and three eager faces looked in at us.

They were all women in their mid-sixties and dressed in their finest wedding outfits.

The tallest woman, who looked remarkably like Gran, squealed and raced over, engulfing Gran in a hug.

"Daphne Chamberlain!" Gran hugged her back.

"Molly! You look amazing." Daphne stepped away and smiled at her.

"You would say that, since we're practically twins."

The other two women raced in and hugged Gran.

Gran was laughing as she took a step back. "Holly, I'd like you to meet three friends of mine. This is Pearl Duchovny, she'll be entertaining us tonight as the singer in the band."

Pearl was curvy, with a magnificent bosom strapped into a red corset dress, her black hair piled on top of her head. She swooped in to give me a kiss.

"This beauty must be your granddaughter," she said.

"That's right," Gran said. "I always had your picture with me and would show you off any time I could."

I grinned. "It's nice to meet you all."

"This is Daphne Chamberlain." Gran introduced me to the woman who'd rushed in first.

"It's a pleasure." Daphne smiled at me.

"And this is Jane Napoleon," Gran said.

I nodded a greeting at her. Jane seemed more formal than the other two. She had perfect posture, was thin, and wore a deep blue linen suit that was crumpled at the elbows.

"You all look familiar," I said, "but I can't place any of you. How do you know my gran?"

Pearl chuckled. "There's a story. Who's going to tell it?"

"We've no time for your long stories, Pearl," Jane said. "Molly's got her wedding to get to. Let's get a move on."

"You don't get to order us around anymore," Pearl said. "We're free women."

Jane's forehead wrinkled. "I never did. I was one of the good ones."

They all laughed, while I looked on in confusion. Why would Jane be ordering them about?

Gran's eyes widened. "Can you believe it? I'm getting married."

"Of course we can," Daphne said. "You always were the prettiest of the group."

Gran laughed again before looking at me. "You probably saw this lot when you visited me in prison. Daphne and Pearl were inmates, and Jane was a guard."

"I'm retired now," Jane said. "But I keep in touch with my ladies. And these three were unforgettable. They always kept me on my toes during my shifts."

"Wow! I didn't know you remained close with anyone from prison," I said to Gran.

"Why not? You make the best friendships on the inside," Pearl said. "You quickly learn who to trust, and who to avoid. I knew Molly was a good 'un the second we met."

"And we bonded because we look so alike and people kept mixing us up," Daphne said. "We pretended we were sisters. We fooled so many people."

"You always pretended, and people believed us," Gran said.

"I'm glad you could all make it," I said. "It should be a fun day."

"It won't be fun for anyone if we hold the bride up any longer," Jane said. "Her groom will think we've kidnapped her."

"Oh! You're right," Gran said. "Come on, ladies, off you go. I'll meet you at the ceremony."

There was a thud on the front door, making Saffron yip.

Daphne groaned. "That'll be Reggie. He was complaining about having to drive us the short distance here to see you."

"You're still dating Reggie Frasier?" Gran's nose wrinkled. "Haven't you gotten rid of him yet?"

"I've tried a couple of times, but he keeps coming back like a bad smell. I'd better calm him down or we'll end up walking back to the castle, and my heels forbid that." Daphne hurried over and opened the door.

A tall, stocky guy with dark hair wearing a black suit stood outside, a scowl on his stubbled face. "We're going to be late. You know I hate being late for things."

"The bride is in here, Reggie. You remember Molly? They can hardly start the wedding without her," Daphne said.

Reggie didn't acknowledge Gran. "If you're not all in the car in the next minute, I'm leaving without you." He turned and stomped away.

"He's as charming as ever," Gran said.

"Ignore him. We had a fight before coming here, and he threatened not to bring me." Daphne shook her head.

"You should find yourself someone new at the reception tonight," Pearl said. "Someone who can put a smile on your face. Weddings always make people romantic."

"As does all the free champagne," Gran said.

Daphne sighed. "It's complicated with Reggie. Come on, ladies, we've held up the bride long enough, and I'm not walking back to the la-de-da castle in these shoes."

There was another flurry of hugs and kisses before they dashed out the door.

I helped Gran touch up her make-up and smoothed down her hair. "You didn't tell me you were inviting anyone from the prison. We looked at your guest list a dozen times, and I don't remember seeing their names on it."

Gran's cheeks flushed. "I didn't want to say anything in case you objected, or were worried they might misbehave."

"I'd never object to you having your friends here, no matter how you got to know each other. From the sounds of it, you looked out for each other when you were inside."

"We did. They're the best girls, and even Jane came in handy now and again. She was one of the more flexible wardens. We had a laugh together, and after she retired, we kept in touch online. I thought she could represent the prison side of my family."

"I'm glad they're here. They seem to make you happy."

"They're entertaining, that's for sure. And Pearl can really belt out a tune. I knew she'd gone back to singing after she got out and had to have her entertain us at the reception. She's really good. She could have been on the

West End stage if she'd kept on the right side of the law."

I caught hold of Gran's shoulders and gave her a gentle squeeze. "I'm happy they're here. Now, no last-minute worries you need to get off your chest before Ray makes an honest woman of you?"

"I'm good. Seeing the girls has helped relax me. I'm ready."

I tucked her hand in my elbow, called for the dogs, and headed to the front door. "Then let's go and get you married."

Chapter 2

"If I have to keep on smiling, my face will crack." Gran spoke through her teeth as we had our photos taken for what felt like the thousandth time by the enthusiastic wedding photographer. "And my shoes are hurting. I thought I'd worn them in enough so they'd be comfortable, but all this standing around is aggravating my bunions."

We were in the beautifully manicured rose garden of Audley Castle, being posed and staged to capture the wedding day.

"I could do with a sit down, too," Ray whispered. "Don't worry, it won't be long before we're enjoying the evening reception."

"I'll definitely need a large glass of champagne or three after this," Gran said.

"Was marrying me so stressful?" Ray kissed her cheek.

"Of course not, you wonderful man. But pinching shoes and backache is no fun."

"That's perfect," the photographer said. "Now I'd like another big group photo. Everyone come in."

It was a medium-sized wedding party. There were thirty people from Ray's family and friends, another twenty from Gran's side, a half-dozen members of staff from the castle, and then Alice and Rupert representing the Audley family.

As the crowd assembled around us, Gran leaned closer. "I know I said not to worry about my prison friends ..."

I slid her a glance. "Is there something you didn't tell me?"

"Well, Pearl's like a magpie. If it sparkles, she wants it. It got her in trouble when she robbed an exclusive jewelry store. She almost got away with it by using an enormous purse and hiding items inside. It wasn't until she walked past the security gate by the door that the alarm rang. She was inside for three years. And that wasn't the first time she'd been caught being light-fingered."

"Okay, so watch her around the family jewelry," I said. "What about Daphne?"

"She wasn't in for anything serious. Some minor fraud. And she only did it because her ex-husband was so tight-fisted she barely had enough money to buy food. But she skimmed a little too much off the top of the business she did the accounts for. The boss discovered what was going on and turned her in. She served eighteen months."

"I take it I don't have to worry about Jane?" I said. "She must be straight down the middle if she was a guard keeping you lot in line."

Gran chuckled. "Don't be so sure. She was one of the more flexible guards, but that came with a price."

"You've lost me." I shuffled closer to Gran as more people crowded around us.

"Jane supplemented her income by doing favors for the prisoners. Nothing big, but she'd smuggle a phone in, or expensive chocolate, sometimes get messages to the outside."

"She was a bent prison warden?"

"Shush, you don't want people overhearing. She was just flexible when it came to the rules. So long as Jane could get something out of it, she'd help you. She did me several favors while I was inside and even got me out of a few scrapes. I consider her a friend."

"Everyone looks perfect," the photographer said. "All eyes on me and give me your best smile."

I forced out another smile, my cheeks also aching. As much as Gran reassured me that her friends wouldn't be a problem, I'd keep a careful eye on them to make sure the evening went smoothly. The Audley family were generous in lending out part of the castle for the wedding and evening reception, and I needed to make sure nothing went wrong.

"That's it for everyone," the photographer said.

There was a collective group sigh as everyone broke apart and moved away.

"I just want another few minutes with the bride and groom."

Gran groaned. "Will this torture never end?"

"You'll be glad you had these photos done so you can look back and remember this day. You'll be so busy, you'll forget most of it." I kissed her cheek. "Go enjoy yourself with Ray. I'll have the champagne waiting for you."

Gran grumbled as she walked away with Ray, following the photographer over to a stunning display of red and yellow roses.

Rupert walked over dressed in a tailored gray suit, his usually messy blond hair neatly brushed off his handsome face, and took hold of my hand. "Have I told you how beautiful you look?"

I grinned at him. "Only five times." I glanced around to make sure Meatball and Saffron were behaving themselves, before walking away from the rest of the wedding party with Rupert.

Even though it had been several months since we'd become an official couple, it always took me a few seconds to get used to not hiding my serious crush on Lord Rupert Audley. Well, it was much more than a crush. I was pretty sure I loved him, but I hadn't told him yet.

"This makes me think of what our wedding day could be like," he said.

I squeezed his hand. "Gran's also mentioned that once or twice. She'll be on our case once her wedding is over."

"Alice is just the same," Rupert said. "She's still talking about organizing the whole thing for us."

"I'm not sure wedding planning is her speciality, but we can always give her one section of the wedding to focus on," I said.

"We could. But you've got to agree to marry me first."

I grinned up at him. "That's very true. I was thinking Alice could organize our honeymoon."

Rupert groaned. "She'll send us to Disneyland."

"I wouldn't mind Disneyland, although I might get sick on the rollercoasters."

"I was thinking somewhere warm with tropical breezes, and big drinks that have umbrellas in them. And just the two of us. Alice has been hinting she wants to come on the honeymoon. I'm not having my sister tagging along and spoiling things."

I laughed. I wouldn't mind Alice coming along, she was great fun. But the honeymoon would just be for us. "If I make her promise not to send us to Disneyland, or anywhere cold, we should give her that job. She'll be so focused on planning the perfect honeymoon that she won't want to take over the rest of the wedding. Then we can have it how we like."

"It does sound like you've accepted my proposal." There was a hopeful look in his eyes. "I can ask you again if you like, just so I know for sure."

Since the first time Rupert had proposed, he'd asked me again three times. Each time, I'd carefully said no, but I was wavering more and more. Everything was great between us, and he was everything I'd hoped for in a boyfriend. He was kind, thoughtful, funny, and sweet. And he wasn't rushing me into anything. I was happy taking my time to get to know everything there was about Rupert Audley.

I slowed and looked out over the vast lake in the castle grounds. This really could be my home for good. It was an exciting prospect.

I opened my mouth to reply to Rupert.

"Holmes! There you are." Campbell Milligan strode over, a stern expression on his face.

"Are you enjoying the wedding?" I asked.

"I wouldn't say enjoying, but it's keeping me busy." Campbell was in charge of the castle security, and my sometime partner in crime solving.

"What's got you on your toes?"

"Your gran failed to mention there'd be criminals among the wedding party. I background checked everyone who planned to attend, and there are several names missing from the list. As soon as I spotted anomalies on the guest list, I got my team to check them out. It's a good job I did. One of your gran's friends has Reggie Frasier as their companion."

"Who's Reggie Frasier?" Rupert said.

"Pearl's date," I said. "I've met Pearl, and she seems nice, although Reggie was grouchy. What's the problem with him?"

"Reggie's a former mobster with a dark past and an even less pleasant present. He's a security risk. He shouldn't be here," Campbell said.

"He didn't come to the wedding to cause trouble, he came because his girlfriend is the singer in the band, and a friend of Gran's. He'll be on his best behavior."

Campbell grunted. "It's not just him I'm concerned about. One of your gran's wedding

party was discovered with some family silverware in her purse."

I grimaced. "I didn't know that. What's happened to her?"

"I'm sure it was a misunderstanding," Rupert
said.

"Lord Rupert, she had candlesticks sticking
out the top of her purse. She was seen on
the CCTV taking them."

"Ah! That is more serious. Did she put them
back?" Rupert said.

"She did," Campbell said. "But that's not—"

"Then everything's fine," Rupert said. "There
was no harm done. And we have plenty of
silver candlesticks. Maybe she thought they
were wedding favors."

Campbell muttered under his breath. "She
should be charged with theft."

"Let's give her the benefit of the doubt," Rupert said. "This is a celebration, and we don't need anything to spoil Molly and Ray's special day. I'm sure you spoke to her and explained the situation about the candlesticks."

"I did. I even suggested she leave."

"No one needs to leave," Rupert said. "These are guests of the bride and groom. Therefore, they stay."

I always got a little swoony around Rupert when he put his foot down. He wasn't often masterful, but I loved it when he was.

"To be on the safe side, perhaps you should set up extra security. We don't want anyone else mistaking expensive family items for party favors," I said.

"That's an excellent idea," Rupert said.

"It's already done," Campbell said. "There won't be any more ... misunderstandings during the wedding reception." He marched off, clearly not happy.

"Thanks for covering for Gran's friend," I said.

"Mistakes happen. Besides, I want this to be a perfect day. Your gran deserves to be happy," Rupert said. "Look! I think the photographer's finally finished with your gran and Ray. We can head to the reception."

I waved at Gran, and she waved back. "She'll be relieved. She's not used to having all this attention on her."

My gaze shifted to Reggie. He stood apart from the rest of the wedding party. He was on his phone, pacing around, a sullen look on his face.

I didn't like to admit it, but like Campbell, I was also a little cautious of Gran's friends, but between us, we'd make sure nothing bad happened. My focus was on making sure Gran and Ray had the best day ever.

"Are you ready for something to eat?" Rupert said.

"Yes, I can't wait. Especially since I wasn't involved in cooking the main meal."

"It must be a treat, having a break from the kitchen," Rupert said.

"I love working there, but it is nice to come to a party I haven't catered for."

"You made the wedding cake," Rupert said. "I heard from Alice that it's incredible."

"It's not bad, if I say so myself." I'd created a four-layer vanilla, maple, and cream tower. Gran had a sweet tooth, so I'd added a glaze of maple drizzle all over it. It had taken me days to complete and was part of my wedding gift to her and Ray.

"Let's go and enjoy ourselves," Rupert said. "But don't forget, my parents will be here soon, and they're looking forward to meeting you. Are you ready?"

"Of course. I'm looking forward to meeting them, too." My stomach clenched at the reminder I'd soon be meeting Rupert's parents, Lord and Lady Audley. They hadn't been to the castle the whole time I'd worked here and had always struck me as elusive, cold, and not all that invested in their children's happiness.

I took several deep breaths as we sauntered back to the castle. I could handle two intimidating members of the Audley family. I solved murders, had put my life at risk when I'd chased down killers, and convinced a lord he loved me. What could go wrong when I met Rupert's parents?

Chapter 3

"Your little dog was adorable when he walked along the aisle." Pearl strolled beside me and Meatball as we headed along the main corridor of the castle. The evening reception was in full swing, and everyone was having a great time.

"He was cute. And he loves a party, so he's in his element with all these new people to make friends with."

Pearl leaned closer. "I have to say, your gran's a lucky lady. Ray's a looker. He must stay in shape with all that gardening. I always like a man with broad shoulders."

I grinned. "They seem very happy together."

She looked around. "I just wish I could find the guy I'm searching for. My guitarist, Jed, is always sneaking off and getting up to things he shouldn't when we go to events. I should put a tracker on him, so I know where he's hiding."

"What do you think he's up to?" My thoughts jumped to the priceless antiques dotted around the castle.

Pearl roared with laughter. "It's not what you think. We're not all criminals."

My cheeks grew warm. I'd been caught out thinking the worst.

"I met Jed once I got out of prison. I was looking for a new guitarist, and he responded to the ad I placed. What he can do with his fingers on those strings is a miracle, but those fingers also like to work their magic on the ladies. They often get giddy with excitement when they learn he's in a band. I always have to keep an eye on him."

I chuckled, still embarrassed for thinking badly of Jed. "You're all amazing. Everyone's been up dancing since you started."

"Thanks. We are fabulous, but we won't be fabulous for much longer if I can't find Jed and get him back on that stage."

I was also looking for someone, but it wasn't Jed. I'd been keeping an eye on Reggie ever since he'd shot pictures of the silverware loaned to the wedding party. After he'd taken his snaps, he'd been on his phone, texting. I was worried he was doing a dodgy deal and hoping to offload the family silverware while everyone was enjoying themselves.

The coat closet door to our left opened. Jed tumbled out, looking like a rumpled version of Mick Jagger. He had lipstick smeared across one cheek and his hair looked thoroughly teased.

"Jed! I should have known you'd be messing around with someone. Get back to the reception. We need to start the next set." Pearl stalked over to him and clouted him on the arm.

"Jeez! Give a guy a break. I was only having fun." He finished buttoning his shirt and grinned at me. "Groupies. What are you gonna do?"

"Keep your man parts inside your pants. That's what you should do. And Holly doesn't want to hear about your latest conquest." Pearl thumped him again. "Focus on stroking your guitar, not the unfortunate woman you left in that closet."

It was hard not to laugh as Jed scuttled off, looking sorry for himself.

"Honestly, he's old enough to know better," Pearl said.

"There's no harm in it, so long as no one gets hurt. And it's a wedding. People tend to cut loose when love is in the air."

She shook her head. "Jed is always cutting loose. I should go. I hope to see you back on the dancefloor soon."

"Of course. I won't be long. Meatball needs a comfort break, then I'll be right back."

Pearl cooed over Meatball for a few seconds, then dashed after Jed, yelling at him.

"But before I can take you outside, we have to find out what Reggie is up to," I said to Meatball.

He gave a quiet woof of agreement.

Reggie had been skulking around the reception all evening. He'd barely touched his food, said hardly a word to anyone, and had a face like thunder all night. He was up to no good, I just knew it. And I wasn't letting him cause any problems on this important day.

Meatball's ears pricked up, and he hurried away. I chased after him, and as I turned the corner, I spotted Reggie. I quietly called

Meatball back, then crept along, making sure Reggie didn't see me. He was pacing again, his phone by his ear.

"Of course I miss you," he said. "But I couldn't get out of this nightmare wedding."

He was missing someone? He was supposed to be Daphne's date. Was he cheating on her?

"I'd leave if I could, but she'd know something was wrong. Besides, I could be onto something sweet here. This castle is crammed full of antiques."

He was planning on stealing! I wasn't letting him get away with that.

"Doll! I wish I could be in your arms right now. I promise, I'll tell her tomorrow. This has been in the diary for ages, and I didn't want to cause a scene." Reggie was quiet for a moment. "Yes, I mean it this time. No more messing you around. As soon as I'm done here, I'll come over. And I'll bring you a gift. Something special."

I frowned. It wouldn't be anything special he'd stolen from the castle if I got my way.

"Put some bubbly on ice, and we'll celebrate when I get back. Just you and me in that new hot tub I got fitted for you. And make sure you wear that yellow bikini I got you. The one with the thong back."

I grimaced. There was nothing worse than a cheater. Or a cheater who thought thongs were sexy. Didn't he know how badly they chafed?

Reggie turned and stared straight at me. "I've gotta go. Something's come up. I'll see you real soon." He ended his call, not taking his gaze from me.

My heart sped up, but I stood my ground. "Hi! You're Daphne's date, aren't you? I'm Holly, the bride's granddaughter."

"I'm happy for you. How much of that conversation did you hear?" He stalked toward me, his eyes narrowed slightly, like he was a predator stalking his prey.

Meatball growled softly as Reggie stopped in front of us.

"It's okay, Meatball. He's a friend. We're all friends here."

"Yeah, we're all friends, so long as you know how to keep your mouth shut," Reggie said. "Don't get me in trouble with Daphne."

"You can only get in trouble if you've done something wrong," I said. "You wouldn't do that to Daphne, would you? She's a nice lady."

"She's a peach. And if I ignore the nagging and wrinkles, she's my ideal woman."

"You're lucky to have her," I said.

He grabbed my arm and squeezed tight. "Let's make sure it stays that way. You keep your mouth shut about what you heard."

I jerked my chin up and met his glare. "Or what?"

Meatball growled again, this time baring his teeth.

"Or you'll find out what I do to people who get in my way," Reggie said.

"Is there a problem, Holly?" Campbell slid from the shadows like an awesome ninja warrior, his tight gaze lasered on Reggie.

Reggie glared at Campbell, then flicked his attention back to me. "There's no problem, is there? Hayley here was talking about the wedding and what a great day she's had. I think she's had too much to drink, though. I was just helping her stay upright."

"It's Holly. And Ronald here was being mean." I yanked my arm out of his grip.

Reggie glowered at me. "You misunderstood. I was being funny." He glanced at Campbell.

"You know how sensitive these women can be."

"I don't. And Holly clearly didn't find your joke amusing," Campbell said. "This area isn't for wedding guests. You need to go back to the reception."

"Sure, sure," Reggie said. "I just have a few more calls to make."

"I hope your calls aren't business-related," I said. "The castle has excellent security, and there are cameras everywhere. I don't want you to make a mistake and pick up a trinket for your other special lady friend that doesn't belong to you."

Reggie clicked his teeth together. "I don't have another special lady friend. Don't go telling lies."

"My security team is all over this place if you're stupid enough to try anything like that," Campbell said.

"You've lost me." Reggie rocked back on his heels.

"Were you lost when you took pictures of the silverware we used at dinner?" I said.

Reggie shrugged. "I took a few pictures of the food to share on my social media accounts. Everyone loves that fancy food stuff online. Why else would I be interested in the knives and forks?"

"That's a good question," Campbell said. "Maybe I'll check your social media profiles, see what you get up to in your spare time."

Reggie raised a hand, a smarmy smile on his face. "I'll go back to the party. The business can wait. And I do have a special lady waiting for me in there. I don't want to disappoint her."

I stood beside Campbell, only shaking slightly as Reggie left.

Meatball gave another bark and then wagged his tail once Reggie had vanished from sight.

"You were very brave," I said to him. "Reggie isn't a nice man."

"What were you doing, stalking a criminal?" Campbell said.

"I had to. He was casing the castle. I'm certain Reggie's been cataloguing things on his phone so he can see if they're worth stealing. I saw him slip out of the reception when the main meal was being cleared away. I reckon he thought he could snoop around because the servers were hurrying back and forth causing a distraction."

"But he didn't know Miss Nosy Parker of the Year was watching him," Campbell said.

"He didn't. I bet he regrets it. He'd be an idiot to steal anything from the castle now he knows we're onto him."

"And my team is onto him. We were moni-toring Reggie on the cameras. If he makes a single wrong move, we'll grab him."

I let out a sigh. "Thanks, Campbell. I just want to make sure everything goes smooth-ly for Gran and Ray."

"It is. The ceremony was great. They both look happy."

"They do. Marriage suits them."

"How about you focus on your gran and Ray and let me deal with the security matters for once?" Campbell's gaze shifted along the corridor. "And I believe you had a hand in making that."

I turned as Chef Heston wheeled my maple glaze and vanilla cake toward the reception.

I sucked in a breath. "I hope Gran and Ray like it."

"They'll love it." Campbell gave me a gentle push. "Go back and have fun and stop seeking out trouble."

I shot him a grin, then hurried over to the trolley and peered at the cake. "Is everything looking good?"

Chef Heston tutted. "I can manage a simple cake delivery. Don't touch it, it's perfect just as it is."

I'd worked hard to recreate the cake design Gran had found. The maple glaze glistened under the lights, and there was a faint shimmer of edible sparkle on the top layer, just as she'd requested.

"Relax, Holly. Your gran will adore this cake. You did a good job. Now, get the door open so I can showcase your creation," Chef Heston said.

I pushed open the door, and he walked through with the cake, which he presented to the top table where Gran and Ray sat.

I hurried in and took my seat, just as Gran stood up. She'd changed out of her wedding dress into a beautiful, pale pink going away outfit for their honeymoon.

She tapped the side of her glass with her fork, drawing everyone's attention. She glanced over at me, and I gave her a discreet thumbs up.

Gran nodded. "I have a long and tangled history with many of you in this room. And I'm sure some of you have memories of me you'd like to forget."

There was a chuckle from the table Daphne, Jane, and Pearl sat at.

"I've always been an independent woman, but I have to admit, I've had my head turned a time or two by the wrong man. I'd just about given up on love when I met this wonderful man beside me." She rested a hand on Ray's shoulder. "He's given me a new passion for life, and even got me into gardening, although the results are mixed. But I have to say, I've never felt happier than when I'm with Ray."

"Same here," Ray said.

"Before I get too emotional, or too tipsy, I have a few thankyous to make. Firstly, to the Audley family, for letting me have my wedding in such a beautiful setting." She nodded at Alice and Rupert, who sat nearby. "Ever since I arrived in this quaint little village, I've met nothing but friendship and openness, especially from this generous, open-hearted family who took me in as if I was one of their own."

Alice raised her glass and nodded at Gran.

"And Ray has worked in the castle grounds for many years, so it was ideal when we were offered the chance to have our wedding here, and use the flowers he'd planted to decorate our surroundings."

Ray looked on proudly at the vases of stunning flowers on the tables.

"I'd also like to thank all the friends and family for making the time to celebrate with us." Gran raised her glass again before turning to me. "Most of all, I'd like to thank my wonderful granddaughter, Holly Holmes. She's stuck by me, no matter how many mistakes I've made. She's kind, determined, and sometimes a little too stubborn for her own good, but her heart is always in the right place. Holly always makes sure she does the right thing and encourages others to do the same. Believe me, she's had to encourage me a fair few times before I saw the right way to live my life, but she never gave up on me."

I shook my head, smiling and dabbing at my eyes. She was my family, and I'd always be there to support her.

"And if she wasn't generous enough with her love and the time she spends with me, she also made our beautiful wedding cake." Gran gestured at the cake in front of her and Ray. "Holly toiled over this for hours to make sure it was perfect. I couldn't be prouder of my talented, wonderful granddaughter." She beckoned me over.

I had to wipe my eyes again before I stood and hugged her.

"You're the best granddaughter a woman could ever want," she whispered in my ear before kissing me on the cheek.

"The same here. I wouldn't change a single thing about you," I said.

Gran kept me by her side as she turned back to the guests. "It's time to cut the cake, stuff our faces with delicious treats, and then start dancing again. Thank you for coming, everyone. Enjoy the rest of the evening."

There was a big round of applause before Gran hugged me one more time and then sat back in her seat.

The cake was moved to the center of the room so everyone could see Ray and Gran as they cut the first slice, then it was taken away to be cut up and handed out to the guests.

Daphne hurried over to Gran, and I did a double take as I spotted her. She was wearing an almost identical outfit, and from the harsh expression on Gran's face, she wasn't happy to see that.

I dashed over and stood beside her. I didn't want Gran causing a scene on her big day.

"Will you look at that." Daphne's voice was high-pitched as her gaze ran over Gran. "I always said you had excellent taste in clothes."

"It's incredible," Ray said. "You both look so alike. Are you sure you aren't related?"

"I'm certain we're not," Gran said, a fixed smile on her face. "Where did you get that outfit, Daphne?"

"I've had this old thing in my wardrobe for ages. I thought it needed an airing. Ray, who do you think is the better looking out of us?"

My eyes widened. She didn't dare just ask that question?

Ray leaned over and kissed Gran's cheek. "My bride is the most beautiful woman in this room."

Gran smiled at him and touched his cheek. "You old romantic."

"You must have a dance with me later," Daphne said to Ray. "Molly's got two left feet, and she'll trample all over you. I'll show you a thing or two on the dance floor."

"Keep your hands off my man," Gran said through gritted teeth.

"I'm sure Daphne's joking," I said.

"That's kind of you to ask," Ray said to Daphne, "but I only have space on my dance card for one woman tonight. Although I may make an exception for Holly, my new grand-daughter."

A warmth spread through me. It was awesome having Ray in my life.

"I'll get you on the dance floor later, just you wait." Daphne laughed and then walked away.

"She's got some nerve," Gran said. "And it's no coincidence we're wearing the same outfit. I sent the ladies a picture of what I was going to wear. I should have known she'd try to best me."

"You look much better than her," I said.

"You look beautiful," Ray said. "I'm the luckiest man alive."

Gran scowled at Daphne as she left the reception room. "She's always trying to outdo me. She even had the same haircut as me when we were in prison. Not that you had much in the way of style options, but she played up our similarities."

"Gran, there's no way Daphne can one up you tonight. You just got married to a wonderful man in an enormous castle."

Gran laughed, and the tension broke. "You're right. Try to beat that, Daphne."

The music started again, and several people took to the dance floor.

"How about we focus on cake and dancing?" I said. "Gran, shall we have a boogie before Ray steals you away for the rest of the night?"

She took my hand and laughed. "You try to stop me."

Chapter 4

I'd been on the dance floor for almost an hour and was glad to take a break. The band was having a rest, but there was music playing in the background to keep the party mood going.

I settled back in my seat and twisted my feet from side to side. I wasn't used to wearing heels, and I'd pay for that over the next few days.

Gran hurried over, not looking happy. "Where's the band? They should have been back ten minutes ago. I don't want my guests getting bored."

"Relax. Everyone's having a great time. And the free bar is keeping people busy."

"Pearl had better not be passed out in a bed-room. She could never hold her drink, and she's been knocking back the free champagne every chance she gets."

"I thought you didn't want to dance anymore because your feet were hurting," I said. "I know mine are."

Gran winced as she lifted one foot. "You're right. I need to sneak off and change my shoes. I've got some pretty flats that'll be perfect for dancing in for the rest of the evening."

"You can't leave the party. Let me get them," I said.

"No, you stay here and enjoy yourself, but cover for me. And make sure Jane doesn't tell Ray all my prison stories. I don't want him to change his mind about marrying me."

"That would be impossible." I laughed as she hurried away. Ray would never do that. He'd barely taken his eyes off Gran since they'd been married. He was smitten, and nothing she did would change his mind.

I gave a contented sigh as I looked around the room. Everyone was enjoying themselves, eating their second piece of cake, drinking wine, and chatting to friends.

Meatball and Saffron bounded past, accepting pats and sneaking pieces of food whenever they got the chance.

The door opened, and the Duchess walked in. She was dressed in a fine dark red gown, a serene expression on her face as she took in the party atmosphere. She spotted me and headed over.

I stood as she approached.

"I hear the party is going well," she said. "Alice brought me a slice of cake earlier, and it was delicious. Was that your creation?"

"It was." I was always pleased when the family enjoyed my food. "Thank you so much for all of this."

"It's our absolute pleasure. The Duke and I get so much enjoyment from Ray's work. And ever since your gran arrived, he's had a spring in his step. I was thrilled to offer them this venue for their special day."

"You and the Duke would be welcome to attend for the rest of the evening," I said. "Although it won't be as fancy as you're used to."

There was a raucous laugh from the other side of the room.

"That's kind of you, but this party is for family and friends. We won't intrude, although if there's any wedding cake left over, I wouldn't say no to another slice or two. The maple glaze was delicious."

"I made four layers of cake, so I'm certain there'll be plenty of leftovers. And Gran will be happy to share some with you."

"Where is your gran? I want to congratulate her on her nuptials."

"You've just missed her. She's changing her shoes into something more appropriate for dancing."

The Duchess smiled as she looked around the room. "I expect this wedding preparation has turned your thoughts to your future with Rupert."

I bit my bottom lip. "A little. It's still early days for us, though."

"Come now, you've known my nephew for a long time. And I've known for almost as long how sweet he's been on you."

I blushed. "You did?"

"Rupert made a terrible job of hiding his feelings." She caught hold of my hand and gently squeezed. "I'm thrilled with the match. But may I give you a few words of caution?"

"Of course. Anything that can help. I know I'm not what his parents would want for his bride."

"You can be sure of that. I don't mean that in any way offensive, but Rupert and Alice's parents have traditional values and beliefs, and they rarely bend them. That was why I was happy when Rupert and Alice came to live with us full time. It gave me an opportunity to open their eyes to the world and see that times have changed. People can do different things, regardless of their birth."

"I know they love living here."

She smiled. "I'm glad to hear that, but the Audley family only bends tradition so much before they put their not insubstantial foot down."

My smile faded. Was this when she told me to leave Rupert alone and that I wasn't good enough for him?

"Oh, don't worry. I'm not sending you to the dungeon for falling in love with Rupert. But I was worried about the match at first."

"Has something been said?"

The Duchess let out a soft sigh. "There were concerns. Not from my side—I know what a kind person you are and how good you've been to Rupert."

"But someone was worried? Rupert's parents?"

She nodded. "However, discovering your advantageous connection to the Mistelthorpes softened them to the idea of you becoming an Audley. I've been pressing that connection home to them."

I wasn't a big fan of only being able to marry someone if you fit the right mold. "That's good to know. But if, and when, Rupert and I make things official, maybe I'll stay a Holmes."

It was still new to me that I had a distant relative with a noble background. And I'd have never found out if it weren't for Alice and her snooping into my family history. Thanks to her, I now had a connection that gave me more legitimacy to become a part of the Audley family. Not that it had ever bothered Rupert where I came from, and I tried not to let it bother me, but these things mattered in certain social circles, and that included the ones Rupert and Alice moved in.

"You need an independent spirit in this family. Don't get lost in all the pomp. It's not as important as some might think. And it isn't all bad, being an Audley. It has many benefits." The Duchess patted my hand. "If you ever have questions, or aren't certain about things, I'm always here."

I gulped. This felt serious. I really could marry into this family. A tingle of excitement ran through me. "That's kind of you. I'm sure I'll have dozens of questions."

"And you can ask any of them. And if you want to stay a Holmes, I'll support that too. We're a modern family these days and must move with the times. Perhaps you could be an Audley-Holmes and have a double-barreled name."

"That has a nice ring to it. I'll give it some thought," I said.

"You do that. And I shall look forward to more of that delicious cake. Enjoy the rest of your evening." The Duchess glided out, nodding and greeting people she passed.

I was glad I had her backing. It meant a lot to me. I'd been intimidated by the grandeur of the Audley family when I'd started working at the castle, but the Duchess had done everything she could to put me at ease. The Duke was another matter, but his behavior wasn't malicious, he just had different interests, mainly involving history and his ancestors' portraits.

A large hand grabbed my elbow, making me jump. I turned to see Campbell.

"What's wrong? Is it Reggie? Did you catch him taking something?"

His hand shook as he gripped me. "It's ... it's not that."

I blinked rapidly. He was pale, sweaty, and it wasn't just his hand shaking, his whole body was quivering.

I hurried him away from any wedding guests to avoid curious stares. "What's the matter? Are you sick?"

He shook his head. "You need to come with me. It's an emergency."

I glanced around before nodding. Campbell almost yanked my arm out of its socket as he pulled me along.

"Slow down! You're scaring me. What's the matter?"

He didn't speak as he hurried me up the staircase and into the guest wing of the castle.

He turned to look at me as he stopped outside a door. "I need your help. I don't know how to fix this."

"Okay. Whatever is wrong, I'm sure we can make it right. But you need to tell me what's going on."

He sucked in a shaky breath and pushed open the door.

I took a step inside the bedroom and stopped. Daphne was lying on the floor in a pool of blood, and Alice was next to her.

Chapter 5

The air felt like it vanished from the room as I took in the scene of Daphne and Alice on the floor.

I gasped, my stomach somersaulting. "Is Alice ... dead?"

Campbell shoved me into the room and shut the door behind him. "No! She's alive, but ... look!" He gestured to Daphne.

A wave of dizziness hit me as I stared with disbelieving eyes, and took a minute to process what I was seeing. Daphne was on her back, fresh blood around her head in a wonky halo. Her eyes were open as she stared at the ceiling. There was a large red mark on the left side of her temple. Next to her, Alice was sprawled out. In one hand, she held a bottle of red wine. The other hand was smeared in blood.

Campbell hadn't moved since he'd shut the door. He was also staring at Alice and Daphne, and breathing so shallowly he'd pass out if he wasn't careful.

I shook the shock from my body and hurried to Alice. I checked her pulse. "Oh! Thank goodness. She's okay. But what happened here?" I leaned over and checked for signs of life on Daphne, but I knew it was too late. There was no pulse. She was gone.

I looked up at Campbell when he didn't reply. "Campbell! Did you see what happened?"

He took a step closer, his focus on Alice. "I came in and found Alice like this. I checked her pulse, then that woman's, then came for you."

This made no sense. "What's Alice doing here?"

Campbell knelt, caught hold of Alice, and held her against his chest. "She can't be involved with this. She'd never hurt anyone." He stroked her hair off her face.

"You shouldn't move Alice. This looks like a murder scene."

"Which she isn't involved in," he said. "Not my Alice. She'd never do anything like this."

"Somehow she's involved, or she wouldn't be lying next to a body. Have you called the police?"

His gaze shot to me. "No! We have to figure out what happened. This must have been a set up. Someone killed this woman and is trying to make Alice look guilty."

"Slow down before you throw out accusations. I need a minute to think. And I know who the victim is," I said. "That's Daphne Chamberlain. She was a friend of my gran's. I don't think she'd met Alice before tonight."

"Which means she had nothing to do with her death," Campbell said. "We don't have to tell the police Alice was in the room. We take her out and hide her somewhere safe until she wakes."

I looked at Alice and then Daphne. I was torn between protecting my dear friend and figuring out what happened to my gran's friend. Although I couldn't see the back of Daphne's head, the blood suggested a serious injury.

But I was right with Campbell. I couldn't believe Alice would hurt Daphne, even though the clues pointed right at her.

"Holly, please! Help me figure this out," Campbell said.

I moved away from Daphne and looked down at Alice. "A woman's been murdered. Do you really want to cover this up? What if someone finds out Alice was moved, or she tells the police something when she wakes?"

"I'm not talking about covering up the whole thing. We'll report Daphne is dead, but we can't let them know Alice was found like this. The blood, the bottle in her hand, the mark on that woman's head. She looks guilty." Campbell kissed Alice's forehead.

She did, but I knew she wasn't. There had to be a way to figure out what went wrong in this bedroom.

Alice groaned. She moved her head from side to side before her eyes blinked open. "Oh! I feel awful. Where am I?"

"Try to stay calm," Campbell said. "There's been an ... accident."

Alice's eyelids fluttered. "I don't feel well. Campbell, what happened to me?"

He looked at me, seeming unable to say any more.

I kneeled next to Alice. "Hey, what have you been up to?"

"Oh, Holly. I didn't see you. I must have done something foolish. Did I trip over again?" Her eyes flickered closed as if she was about to go to sleep.

"Don't you remember what happened?" I said.

She sniffed and her nose wrinkled. "There's a strange smell in here. Metallic. I don't like it. It reminds me of a butcher's store."

Campbell looked at me and lifted his shoulders.

I had no explanation to give. If Alice didn't remember how she got here, neither of us could help her.

"Can you stand?" Campbell said.

"I'm not sure that's a good idea," I said. "We haven't made a decision about what to do yet."

"What are you deciding on?" Alice said. "I have to admit, I quite like being in Campbell's arms, I just wish I could remember how I got here."

"I know what needs to happen. Alice must leave here immediately," Campbell said. "You can see there's something wrong. She could have been killed."

"Killed? I ... why? And why do I feel so strange?" Alice said.

"Try to focus," I said. "What's the last thing you remember before you passed out?"

"I passed out?"

"Holly! We don't have time for this," Campbell muttered.

"We can spare a couple of minutes. Alice, think carefully. Do you remember what happened? Did you faint?"

Her gaze shifted from Campbell to me. "I don't think so. The last thing I remember clearly was being at the wedding reception."

"Who were you talking to?" I said.

"Everyone. I was getting to know all your gran's wonderful friends. And Ray's family are so sweet, just like him. I felt hot, so thought I'd get some air. Then everything gets fuzzy." Her gaze flicked around. "I'm in a bedroom, so I must have come upstairs, but this room isn't mine."

"Let's get you out of here," Campbell said. "Focus on me. Don't look anywhere else. There's nothing to worry about."

"I'm not worried, just confused. And I like looking at you very much, but I know you're not telling me the whole truth, Campbell," Alice said. "What's in this room with us? Answer me. You're both hiding something. I insist you tell me what's happening."

"It's nothing for you to worry about," he said. "Holly and I have everything in hand. You need to rest. Maybe you're getting sick, or you're over-excited because of the party."

"I'm neither of those things, but I did eat too much cake," Alice said. "Although that's never made me faint before." She gripped Campbell's arms as he helped her to her feet.

"Take your time." He handled her like she was made of glass.

"What's that on my hand?" Alice stared at her bloody palm.

"Nothing! Let me wipe that off for you," Campbell said.

"You shouldn't do that." I understood why Campbell wanted Alice out of the room, but he was seriously messing with a crime scene. This could come back to bite him on the behind.

Alice sniffed her palm. "Is this blood? Have I cut myself?"

"No, that blood isn't yours," I said.

"Holly, don't you dare say any more," Campbell said.

"Campbell, let go of me. What aren't you telling me?" Alice turned to me. Her gaze shifted over my shoulder and the color in her cheeks drained away. "Is that ... a body?"

I caught hold of her elbows as she swayed. "Take a deep breath. We found you in this room unconscious, and you were next to a woman's body."

"I was? I ... I have no memory of that. She looks familiar."

"Forget you were even here," Campbell said. "I'll take you to your room so you can clean up and rest."

"Forget I was here?" Alice said. "Maybe I can help. I might have seen something. I could have fainted in shock."

"Do you remember that?" I said.

Alice scrubbed at her forehead. "No, I don't even remember coming into this room. You don't think I had anything to do with this, do you?"

"You didn't," Campbell said. "Like you said, you most likely saw something bad happen and it upset you. Now, I'm taking you out of here. Don't say another word about this until we figure things out. There'll be an explanation for why you were in here."

Alice looked at the body again. "I'm not sure I can walk. My legs feel funny and my head is pounding."

Campbell scooped Alice into his arms. "Hold on tight. I'll take you back to your room."

He was almost to the door when it was flung open.

Lady Philippa rushed in, her eyes wide and her hands fluttering in front of her. "I'm too late! I should have warned you about this. Oh! Is Alice okay?"

"I feel funny, Granny," Alice said. "And there's a dead woman in the bedroom."

"I'm taking Princess Alice back to her room," Campbell said. "She's had a shock."

"Of course. Alice, try not to panic." Lady Philippa hurried over to me as Campbell strode away with Alice in his arms.

"Did you have a prediction about this murder?" I asked.

Lady Philippa looked down at Daphne and grimaced before nodding. "I was having such a fun time that I got distracted. I kept feeling odd, but ignoring it. I ate so much rich food at the wedding and thought it must be that upsetting me. I missed the signs. Then I got a blinding image. Alice was on the floor and there was a lot of blood. I panicked and thought she'd been harmed."

"Alice will be okay, but when Campbell found her next to Daphne, she was unconscious. She was also holding what might be the murder weapon." I pointed at the wine bottle that had rolled away when Campbell moved Alice.

Lady Philippa shook her head. "We know Alice would never do this, but what has she got herself tangled in?"

"Did your vision give you any clues about who could be involved?"

"I panicked when I got the image and almost jumped out of my skin when I focused. I thought it was your gran who'd been killed. Then I looked around the reception and saw her standing next to Ray, so I was confused. I've been searching the rooms, trying to find Alice to see if my vision was correct."

"You didn't see Daphne's attacker? It looks like she's been hit over the head with something hard."

"My visions are never that helpful," Lady Philippa said. "I didn't see anyone other than Alice and ... Daphne?"

"Yes, my gran's friend. You said Alice was in your vision too. What was she doing?"

Lady Philippa's hand shook as she pressed it against her breastbone. "She looked dead. And when I saw Campbell carrying her just now, I thought that had come true. I don't understand what she was doing in here."

"Neither do I, but that's what we need to figure out."

Lady Philippa was quiet for a moment as she looked around the room. "I don't want Alice involved in this crime, but was Campbell right to take her away? He could have disturbed evidence."

"I don't think he was right to move her, but he's so protective of Alice that he's not thinking straight."

She bit her bottom lip. "We have to do the right thing. Daphne is dead, and someone killed her."

I nodded. "We need to stop any more evidence being contaminated."

"We should shut this room up and call the police." Lady Philippa gave a determined nod. "I don't like it any more than you do that Alice was found next to a body, but no one will believe she's involved in a murder."

"You're right. I'm sure when she's calmed down, she'll remember why she was in here. She could even remember who attacked Daphne."

Lady Philippa followed me out of the room, and I turned and shut the door.

"Oh! I've just had a terrible thought. Has anyone told your gran what's happening?"

I closed my eyes for a second. "No, she won't know about this, but she'll find out as soon as the police turn up. I'd better tell her before they arrive."

"You deal with the police, I'll go and speak to your gran. We've become close since she moved here. It's the least I can do to help." Lady Philippa gave me a brief hug before hurrying away.

I looked back at the closed door and sighed. Gran and Ray's wonderful wedding would be ruined by this news, and my best friend looked like she was a murder suspect. Add in the fact my usually reliable sidekick had fallen apart because the love of his life looked like a killer, and I had a big problem on my hands.

Chapter 6

The wedding celebrations quickly wound down as soon as the police showed up. The guests went back to their hotels or to the rooms they were using in the castle, and the once cheerful, fun-filled atmosphere felt tense and pensive.

I looked out the window opposite Alice's bedroom and rubbed my eyes. It was the early hours of the morning, and I hadn't sat down for hours as the events of the evening unfolded. The police had examined the crime scene, confirming it looked like foul play, and Daphne's body had been taken away for further examination.

It wouldn't be long before the questions began, and I wasn't certain how to handle those.

The doctor who served the family came quietly out of Alice's room.

I hurried over, Meatball glued to my ankle. "How's Alice doing?"

He turned and nodded. "She's comfortable, and she asked to see you."

"Of course." I moved to the door, but he put a hand on my arm.

"Be gentle with her, she's in shock. And when I first attended to Princess Alice, she seemed woozy."

"Woozy? Did she tell anything else?" I hadn't had a chance to speak to Alice since the discovery of Daphne's body. I had no idea what had been discussed.

The doctor pursed his lips. "She did. She's very concerned about being found with a body."

I gulped. The secret was out. "Oh, yes! She must be."

He waited for me to keep talking, but I didn't want to get Alice or Campbell in any trouble.

"Perhaps it was something she ate or drank that made her feel strange," I said.

The doctor frowned. "I've taken blood samples to check for any abnormalities. Try not to worry. But Princess Alice would appreciate a friendly face. Don't stay too long. I've given her a sedative, so she'll fall asleep soon."

"I'll only stay a few minutes, just to make sure she's settled."

He nodded at me and headed along the corridor.

I slipped into Alice's room and walked to her bed. The room was a mixture of pastels and luxurious throws and cushions.

"Holly, thank goodness. I thought the doctor would never leave. He kept prodding me about and asking questions. I'm so glad you're here." She caught hold of me with one hand

and petted Meatball with the other when he jumped on her bed.

"Have you got your memory back?" I gave her hand a squeeze.

"No! I wish I knew what was happening. I was hoping you could help me fill in the blanks."

I settled on the edge of her bed. "I can only tell you what I saw when I entered the room."

She nodded, her eyes wide. "Which was?"

"You on the floor next to Daphne."

Alice let out a sigh. "Everything is a horrible blur. I keep trying to remember how I got in that guest bedroom with that ... body." She shuddered. "The last clear memory I have is of being in the corridor downstairs. I was thinking I needed to change because I was overheating. Then I think I saw someone and wanted to speak to them."

"Who did you see?"

"I'm not sure. Someone I knew. I was heading up the stairs, and ... that's it! It's so frustrating. I definitely don't remember seeing a body." She yanked me closer. "How's your poor gran doing? She must be feeling terrible."

"She's not great. But Lady Philippa has been wonderful with her. She told her the news about Daphne."

"Her wedding has been spoiled." Alice shook her head. "I have to remember so we can figure out what happened." She gave a huge yawn.

"We will. Maybe after you've slept."

"No, we must do it now. I won't be able to sleep while this is churning in my thoughts." Alice covered her mouth as she yawned again.

"Let's start at the beginning while your eyes are still open. You don't remember how you got in the bedroom, but did you see anyone in the corridor outside the room, or on the stairs? Anyone acting oddly?"

"No one like that. But as I said, the memories leading up to me getting in that room are blurry."

"Have you ever met Daphne before?"

"No, not until the wedding," Alice said. "I made a point of introducing myself to all your gran's friends. I know coming to the castle can be scary and wanted to make sure everyone was comfortable. Daphne was so friendly. She even gave me a hug. She seemed like a nice lady. Who would want to kill her?"

"That's what we'll find out. What did you talk about?"

"The usual things. The castle, how nice everyone looked, and that we were all looking forward to the dancing." Alice thumped a hand on the pink bedspread. "I feel like I'm missing something important. Something that'll help solve this. Why was I next to Daphne when I woke? Why did I have her blood on my hand?"

I needed to come clean with Alice. The police had sealed the room Daphne had been found in and taken any incriminating evidence, and that included the bottle of wine. The bottle that would have her fingerprints on. And that would lead to tricky questions from the police.

I opened my mouth but didn't know where to start. There was no easy way to tell your best friend she was about to be in the limelight for all the wrong reasons.

Her eyes narrowed. "What are you keeping from me, Holly? I tried to get Campbell to tell me what was going on, but he was hopeless. He kept telling me not to worry, and he'd fix everything. He said he'd make sure nothing bad happened to me."

I pulled back my shoulders. She needed to know the truth, especially since Alice had revealed to the doctor that she'd seen Daphne's body. "Campbell found you in that room with Daphne. You were unconscious next to her."

"He told me that. What else?"

"From what I saw of the body, Daphne was hit at least twice on the head with something heavy. She had a red mark on her temple, but no open wound."

"So that didn't kill her?"

"She could have been struck on the back of the head, too. She was hit from behind first, then turned to face her attacker and was struck again."

"How awful. But ... what does that have to do with me being in the room?"

I cleared my throat and took a deep breath. "Alice, you had your hand on a bottle of wine. It's possible that was the murder weapon."

She opened her mouth, then closed it. "I ... I was holding the murder weapon?"

"I don't know for sure, but a bottle would have been heavy enough to inflict those injuries on Daphne. I don't know, maybe you came into the room and disturbed the killer. You saw the bottle on the floor and went to pick it up, but passed out in shock. Could that have happened?"

Alice was silent, chewing on her bottom lip. "I don't remember anything like that happening, I really don't. And I'd tell you if I ran into a killer and he fled, I'd be bursting with pride. Well, I'd rather I found him before the murder happened, but you know what I mean. I could have stopped him."

"I could be wrong about the bottle." I really hoped I was wrong.

"It seems too much of a coincidence it was there," Alice said. "And I don't make a habit of wandering around with bottles of alcohol, so I doubt I brought it into the room."

"Daphne could have had it with her. She could have snuck it off a table at the reception to have later with her boyfriend."

"What about the blood on my hands?" Alice's voice was almost a whisper. "Why would that be there if I wasn't involved?"

"You could have tried to help Daphne," I said. "You went in the room, found her, and tried to revive her."

"Yes, that's possible. I always try to help when I can." Alice looked down at her folded hands. "Holly, you don't think I'm the killer?"

"Alice, no! Not for a second. And neither does Campbell."

She blinked swiftly several times. "That's good. Because without my memory, I may have done it and simply don't remember."

Angry voices outside the room had us both turning to the door. Meatball barked and jumped off the bed. There was a yell and something heavy thudded against the wall.

"What's going on out there?" Alice said. "That sounded like Campbell shouting."

"You wait here. I'll go take a look." I hurried to the door and pulled it open.

Campbell had a uniformed police officer pinned against the wall, his face a mask of rage. "You can't stop me from seeing her."

"Campbell, what are you doing?" I hurried out of the room with Meatball and closed the door behind me so Alice wouldn't see the fight.

"I need to see Princess Alice," he said. "This idiot said I can't go in. I have to know how she's doing."

"Calm down! Alice is doing better. She's still confused, but we're figuring things out. The doctor's been to see her, and I've just been talking to her."

The police officer struggled in Campbell's grip. "I'll have you arrested for assault."

"Let him go," I said to Campbell. "You can't be of any help to Alice if you end up behind bars."

Campbell heaved out a breath before slowly releasing the police officer.

"Put your hands behind your back," the officer said.

"There's no need to arrest Campbell. He's just worried about his friend."

"I don't care. He attacked me. Hands behind your back," the police officer said again.

Campbell didn't move as tension radiated off him.

"I can add resisting arrest to your list of offences if I have to."

I didn't recognize the police officer, which was unusual. Campbell and the security team had a decent working relationship with them, but this guy didn't seem to understand that. Or if he did, he didn't care.

I stepped forward. "You must be new. I'm Holly. I work at the castle."

The officer slid me a glare. "Sergeant Rochford."

"It's nice to meet you. Campbell is in charge of the security around here. Your boss has probably mentioned him. He can be a hot head, but he's basically decent. And I'm sure he's sorry for being rough with you."

Campbell grunted and flexed his hands.

Sergeant Rochford scowled at me. "I know all about the special privileges the security team gets, and I'm not happy with it. Especially not if this guy is covering something up."

Uh, oh! Word was getting around about Alice being found with Daphne's body.

"Campbell wouldn't cover up anything important," I said. "He's always thorough and professional."

"I don't have time for this," Campbell said. "I need to see Princess Alice."

Sergeant Rochford dodged in front of the door. "Back away and calm down, or you're not getting in to see anyone."

Campbell glowered at him and took a step closer.

"Maybe you should do what he says," I muttered at Campbell.

But he was too angry and too focused on getting to Alice to listen to me. He strode to the door and tried to shove past Sergeant Rochford.

Sergeant Rochford wasn't a small guy, and he shoved back.

Campbell swung a punch, and it connected with a loud crack.

Sergeant Rochford yelled and slammed back against the wall, one hand clutching his jaw.

"Campbell Milligan! Stop that disgraceful behavior this instant." The Duchess strode along the corridor.

Campbell instantly backed away, the fight draining from him as his shoulders slumped.

I tried to help Sergeant Rochford to his feet, but he brushed me away, bright dots of color on his cheeks. "That's it, you're definitely under arrest now."

The Duchess arrived, and from the tight expression on her face, she wasn't happy by what she'd seen. "I'm so sorry, officer." She turned to Campbell. "Not only are you under arrest, you're also suspended from duty."

Campbell jerked upright. "No! Princess Alice needs me."

"You're not fit for duty," the Duchess said. "Since you can't control your temper, you can't work here, or be around Alice. I understand this is a highly charged situation, but you've gone too far by striking an officer of the law."

Campbell's gaze cut to the bedroom door.

"And you're not to go in and see Alice." The Duchess's words rang with authority. "Your suspension begins immediately. I don't want to see you back here until this matter is resolved. If you do return, you'll never work at the castle again. Have I made myself clear?"

"Campbell," I muttered under my breath, shaking with surprise at the anger in the Duchess's voice. She meant business.

"I understand," Campbell said. "I just want to do the right thing by Princess Alice."

"Then go with this officer and explain yourself," the Duchess said. "We have a reputation to maintain, and it does not involve brawling with members of our police."

The bedroom door cracked open, and Alice's pale face appeared. "What's happening out here? Who's being arrested?"

The Duchess rushed over and pushed the door wider before hugging Alice. "There's nothing to concern yourself with. The situation got a bit tense, but everyone is fine."

"Is Campbell in trouble?" Alice said. "I'm sure he was only trying to protect me. And ... And I think I've done something stupid."

"Princess Alice, don't say another word," Campbell said.

"You can say whatever you like. I'm interested in what you have to confess," Sergeant Rochford said.

Campbell growled and looked like he was about to punch him again.

"Campbell, it's time you left," the Duchess said. "Although I would appreciate your recommendation as to whom I can put in charge while your suspension is active."

"Saracen will keep things ticking over." Campbell glanced at me.

I gave him a discreet nod. I worked well with Saracen and considered him a good friend. He'd help me figure out this mess with Alice, clear her name, and make sure Campbell got out of trouble as quickly as he could so he could also help.

"Campbell's been suspended?" Alice pushed away from the Duchess and staggered toward him. "What happened?"

"Don't worry about me." Campbell's expression softened. "You just look after yourself."

The Duchess caught hold of Alice's arm and gently tugged her back. "You need to go to bed and rest."

"She needs to answer the questions we have for her," Sergeant Rochford said. "They're crucial to this investigation."

"What questions does Princess Alice have to answer?" Campbell said. "What are you suggesting she's done?"

Everyone focused on Sergeant Rochford.

He cleared his throat. "We've been gathering information, and the princess was seen entering the victim's bedroom."

I stifled a gasp, while Alice let out a sob. There was no way we could keep her involvement a secret now.

The Duchess hugged her again. "It's nothing to worry about, but the police will need to speak to you. You could have seen something useful."

"But not now," I protested. "Alice has had a shock, and the doctor gave her something to calm her nerves. Can't the questions wait 'til the morning? Surely, you can speak to other people, or look over the body, or do something else. Alice needs to rest. She won't go anywhere."

"I promise, I won't, and I am feeling woozy," Alice said, throwing me a grateful glance.

Sergeant Rochford glared at Campbell. "I do have something else to deal with, but I'll be back first thing in the morning. Let's move." He marched away with Campbell in front of him.

Alice swiped her damp eyes with the back of a hand. "Everything is going wrong. Campbell's been arrested, I can't remember if I killed that lady, and I've ruined the wedding."

"You haven't ruined anything," I said. "And you're innocent. Your memory will come back once you've slept and are less stressed."

Lady Philippa and Rupert appeared at the end of the corridor, Rupert holding Lady Philippa's elbow as she hurried toward us.

"What are you doing up so late?" the Duchess said. "You should have gone to bed hours ago."

"I can't sleep with all this going on," Lady Philippa said. "Alice, you poor girl. How are you holding up?"

"Not great, Granny," she said. "And now they've taken Campbell. What am I supposed to do without him?"

"What's he got to do with this?" Lady Philippa said.

"He hit a police officer," I said.

Her eyebrows whizzed up. "I miss all the fun."

"Let's get you back to bed," the Duchess said to Alice. "Things will seem better in the morning. Everyone else should go to bed, too." She led Alice into her room and closed the door.

"How's my gran doing?" I said to Lady Philippa.

"She put on a brave face while saying good-bye to her wedding guests. It helped she had Ray with her."

I hadn't had a chance to see Gran since this whole mess began. I looked at Alice's bedroom door. I wanted to stay and help her, but I needed to check on Gran.

"We'll be fine here," Lady Philippa said. "Go and be with your family and make sure your gran is okay. I'm sure she'd appreciate you being around."

"Thanks, I will. But I'll be back in the morning. And the police are keen to talk to Alice."

"They're foolish if they think she's involved in this murder," Lady Philippa said.

"She still has no memory of how she got in the bedroom with Daphne, and she's worried she did something bad."

"There's nothing you can do right now. Let me take you home," Rupert said.

"What about Lady Philippa?" I said.

She waved us away. "I'll be fine. I want to check in on Alice before I turn in."

After saying goodbye to her, I walked along the corridor with Rupert and Meatball, headed back down the stairs, and walked out the main castle doors.

My head was spinning with everything that had happened this evening. Alice must be terrified. Campbell was her silent, faithful rock, and he'd just been ripped away from her. She had to remember what happened.

"How are you doing?" Rupert said.

"I think I'm almost as shocked as Alice. I want to wake up and for this to have been a nightmare."

He gently pinched me. "It's happening, but we both know Alice. She can be a proper idiot at times but doesn't have a malicious bone in her body. And I know you, Holly. You'll find out what happened to my sister."

I grabbed his hand and held on tight. "I promise, I will." This had been a horrible end to a wonderful evening, but at least it couldn't get any worse.

Rupert tipped his head. "There's a car coming."

I turned to see a large, sleek black limousine with personalized number plates.

"Oh! It can't be. They're here early." Rupert stared at the limo.

"Who is it?" I said.

"It's my parents."

I inwardly groaned. What had I been saying about things not getting any worse?

Chapter 7

A shudder ran through me as I shifted from foot to foot, while Rupert approached the limousine as it stopped outside the castle. This was the last thing I needed, meeting his parents when I had something crucial to focus on. I wanted to make a good impression, but how could I do that when I had to concentrate on a murder?

The limousine driver opened the back door, and Lord and Lady Audley stepped out.

"This is a nice surprise. We didn't expect a welcoming party so late," Lady Audley said.

"Mother! What are you doing here?" Rupert said.

"You silly boy, you knew we were coming." She turned her cheek so he could kiss it. Lady

Audley was tall and slender, with pale blonde hair cut into a stylish, graduated bob. She wore a tailored coat in a soft gray fabric, and her fingers glittered with jewels.

"I expected you this afternoon. That was the plan." Rupert turned and shook hands with his dad, who was also blond with a long, refined face and a Roman nose.

"We got an earlier flight. Your father has business in London and he wanted to do some work before traveling there." His mother looked up at the castle. "What's going on? Why is the castle lit up so late?"

Rupert looked over at me. "I, um, about that. There's been an incident. Before I tell you about that, I'd like you to meet—"

"Has there been a wedding?" his dad said. "There is confetti on the gravel."

"Yes. A member of our staff was married today. They had their wedding here," Rupert said. "Forget the wedding. There's someone I'd—"

"The party is still going on? It's awfully late," his mother said.

Rupert sighed. "That's not why all the lights are on. You should come inside, I've got some bad news."

"It's not your sister?" his mother said. "Has she done something silly again?"

"It does involve Alice." Rupert looked over and gestured at me to join him.

I couldn't avoid it any longer. I plastered a smile on my face and walked over.

"Mother, Father, before I tell you what's going on, I'd like you to meet Holly Holmes."

His mother's head jerked toward me, and her gaze ran over me. "You're dressed up for someone who works in the kitchen."

"Mother! We talked about this," Rupert said. "Holly's my girlfriend. It doesn't matter where she works."

It looked like it mattered very much to Lady Audley. I didn't know whether to curtsy or hold out my hand to be shaken, so I simply stood there. "My gran got married today. I was the bridesmaid, that's why I'm all dressed up. It's nice to meet you both."

Lady Audley lifted her chin a fraction. Was that disdain or disappointment in her eyes? "Are you involved in this incident with Alice?"

"The ... incident has nothing to do with Holly." Rupert turned and looked at his dad. "Father, aren't you going to say anything? This is Holly, my future wife, if she'll have me."

"I heard you," his dad said. "I'll be inside. You can catch me up on the details later. Alice had better not have made a fool of herself, or she'll be back in finishing school. Again."

I barely held in my snort of surprise. Lord Audley was so dismissive. He didn't seem at all happy to see Rupert, the son he barely saw from one year to the next, and he knew something was going on with Alice, but didn't care what it was. What kind of family was I considering marrying into?

I looked at Rupert and my heart softened. A kind family. I loved Rupert and Alice, and I adored Lady Philippa. His parents just needed time to warm up to me. Plus, they must be tired after traveling so late at night. I needed to give them the benefit of the doubt.

Rupert's dad stopped as he reached the entrance to the castle. "Just in case there are any problems, I'll get Peterson on the case in the morning. He always sorts out these little issues Alice gets herself into." He headed inside without another word.

"Who's Peterson?" I said.

"The family lawyer," Rupert said. "He's very good. It's not a bad idea to have him here."

"I'm sure this won't require legal intervention, whatever it is," his mother said.

Meatball raced around from the side of the castle and bounded over to Lady Audley, wagging his tail.

She took a step back, then her stern expression morphed into a warm smile. "How delightful. Who does this little chap belong to?"

"He's mine," I said. "His name is Meatball. He goes almost everywhere with me."

"Rupert mentioned you had a dog. He's charming." Lady Audley petted Meatball's head, and he rolled onto his side to accept a belly rub.

She laughed. "I expect he spends a lot of time with the Duchess's dogs."

"Um, not really. They're more rivals than friends," I said.

"Well, I think he's wonderful. I'd love to have dogs, but with all the traveling we do, they wouldn't like it." Her gaze settled on me again, and the warmth left her face as if she remembered who I was and wasn't impressed. "Come along, Rupert. You'd better get me up to speed on what's going on with Alice."

Rupert nodded before touching my elbow. "Holly, if you don't mind, I'd better deal with this."

"Of course not. I need to get back to Gran anyway and see how she's doing."

Lady Audley turned back to me. "Miss Holmes, we should spend some time together. Join us for breakfast tomorrow. We can discuss your future plans."

I looked at Rupert and gave a slight shake of my head. I had a murder to investigate. I didn't have time to make Rupert's parents happy. But if I didn't spend time with them, they'd never accept me as a potential daughter-in-law.

"I hope that won't be a problem with your busy schedule in the kitchen," Lady Audley said. "I'm sure the chef can spare you. Or are you really that indispensable?"

"Holly's indispensable to me," Rupert said, a pleading look in his eyes.

I couldn't let him down. "You're right. We do need to get to know each other properly. Breakfast sounds great."

"Are you sure?" Rupert said. "What about..." He inclined his head at the castle.

"I can make the time. It's no trouble."

"I'm so glad to hear we aren't any trouble to you," Lady Audley said. "Until tomorrow."

Rupert kissed my cheek before taking his mother's outstretched arm and walking her into the castle, the picture of formality.

I blew out a breath. That could have gone worse, and I was grateful for Meatball saving the day. At least that was one good thing about Lady Audley. Anyone who liked animals couldn't be all bad.

I dashed back to my apartment, my heels protesting as I crunched through the gravel. I hurried through the front door with Meatball by my side.

Ray hopped up from his seat on the couch and strode over.

I gave him a quick hug. "How's Gran doing? Sorry, I should have been here earlier, but I got caught up in everything at the castle."

"Don't worry about her. I've been keeping an eye on things." He led me back into the lounge. "And she's just fallen asleep, so it's probably best not to disturb her."

I sank into a seat, the exhaustion of the evening finally catching up with me. "She must be feeling terrible."

"She's in shock and keeps saying she can't believe it. She was telling me that Daphne was always the tough one and wouldn't have wanted to go out like this."

"Poor Gran. I feel terrible for her. And on your wedding day."

"It's not the best timing." He patted my hand. "Let me make you some tea. I expect you've been through the wringer as well. I heard Princess Alice found Daphne. How is she?"

"Thanks, tea would be great." Ray headed into the kitchen, but it was only a small place, so it was easy to carry on our conversation. "Alice is confused. This whole situation is confusing."

"You can relax for a while now. There's nothing to be done in this late hour. Do you want anything in your tea? Your gran always likes a nip of whiskey in hers when she's had a rough day."

I smiled. He was right, and it was usually more than a nip. "No, just strong tea will be great." I leaned back and closed my eyes. How was Alice involved with this? Maybe she'd been injured if she'd fought with Daphne. But had there even been a fight? And what was it about? I hadn't seen evidence of a scuffle in the room, just Daphne and Alice with a possible murder weapon in her hand.

And I was still digesting the way Alice's parents seemed so disinterested in learning what was going on with their own child. It made no sense to me. None of this did.

The sounds from the kitchen drifted away as another wave of exhaustion hit me. I'd just close my eyes for five minutes, drink my tea, and then get investigating.

I jerked upright and blinked my bleary eyes. I groaned. I'd fallen asleep on the couch. A blanket covered me.

I'd only meant to have five minutes, and planned to spend the night puzzling through what had happened in the castle, but the bright morning sky peeking through the curtains showed me I'd slept the whole night through.

Meatball lay across my feet, gently snoring.

I was still in my bridesmaid's dress. It wasn't the most comfortable thing to sleep in, and my neck was aching from being on the couch.

I shuffled my feet out from under Meatball, gave him a quick stroke, and then let him out to do his business.

While he was outside, I filled his food and water bowl, and then headed into the bathroom for a quick shower and a change into more appropriate clothes.

As I opened the bathroom door, there were sounds coming from the kitchen.

I hurried into the kitchen, roughly drying my wet hair, to find Gran by the sink in her leopard print dressing gown.

Saffron was next to her, begging for treats.

I rushed over and hugged Gran. "How are you doing this morning?"

She gave me a tight hug back. "I didn't think I'd sleep, but the excitement of yesterday and then everything that happened with Daphne got to me. Ray put me to bed with a hot toddy and I passed out."

"Where's Ray?"

"He was fussing around me this morning and getting in my way, so I sent him to check on the remaining wedding guests. Some have rooms in the castle, and the rest are at the hotel." She shook her head. "What must they think, coming to our wedding, and a guest being killed?"

"I'm so sorry about Daphne." I led her to the kitchen table, and we both sat.

Gran stood straightaway, making Saffron yip with excitement, and hurried to the fridge. "I need something comforting." She walked back with a layer of her wedding cake in her hands.

I smiled as she cut two large pieces and passed me one.

Meatball and Saffron sat beside the table with hopeful looks on their furry faces. I grabbed them each a meaty chew to keep them occupied while we talked.

"This cake is too delicious to go to waste, and I need something sweet for the shock. I'm sure you do, too." Gran took a bite of her cake. "How's Alice? I couldn't believe it when I heard she was found in the room with Daphne. Were they attacked by the same person?"

"I'm not sure Alice was attacked." I scooped up a piece of maple glazed icing on my finger and licked it off. "Have the police spoken to you?"

"Only for a few minutes. They asked me who I was, where I lived, and what my connection was to Daphne."

"They didn't tell you anything about Alice?"

"No. I assumed that whoever killed Daphne went after Alice too." Gran tilted her head. "Is that not what happened?"

"I ... I'm not sure. Alice and Daphne were the only two people found in the bedroom. Alice was unconscious."

"I didn't realize she'd been hurt."

"No, I don't think she was hurt, but she was next to Daphne, and ... she had a bottle of wine in her hand."

"She was passed out drunk? That doesn't seem like an Alice thing to do. She enjoys her bubbles, but I've never seen her get silly with too much drink."

"The police think Alice may be involved with what happened to Daphne." I lifted a hand as Gran sucked in a breath. "Which I don't believe for a second, but when I entered the room and saw them together, it didn't look good."

Gran swallowed her piece of cake and licked her lips. "This has to be a mistake. Alice Audley killing my friend Daphne, I can't believe that."

"I'm glad you said that. I'd hate you to think badly of Alice. She's so confused about what happened. She can't remember why she was in that room, or even going in to see Daphne. She doesn't even remember fainting and has no recollection of the bottle of wine."

"Hold on, the police think this bottle of wine was the murder weapon?"

"It's possible," I said. "They haven't said anything outright, but if I was them, that's exactly what I'd be thinking."

"Someone else must be involved," Gran said.

"They have to be. Can you think of anyone who had a problem with Daphne?" I said. "Anyone at the wedding yesterday who'd want to kill her?"

Gran pursed her lips, her eyes slightly narrowed. "Daphne's always been feisty, and sometimes people didn't like that, but there was no one there I'd consider her enemy."

There was a knock at the door, and I hopped up and opened it.

Saracen stood outside. He glanced at me and looked away. "Sorry to bother you, but I need to speak to your gran. Is she around?"

"Hey, Saracen. Sure, she's right here. How's everything going with the investigation?"

He lifted one shoulder as he stepped inside. "It's going. I didn't get much sleep last night." He nodded at my gran. "Morning, Molly. Sorry to come here unannounced, but I need to ask you a few questions about what happened last night."

"I was doing just that," I said. "Join us for a cup of tea or coffee?"

Saracen rubbed the back of his neck. "No, I'd better not. This is a formal visit."

"You are being very official. I hope you don't think I'm a suspect in this murder," Gran said with a smile on her face.

"The police won't think that," I said. "You were the bride. Everyone's attention was on you yesterday. You couldn't have committed a murder. And that eager photographer was snapping away throughout the reception. He'd have caught you."

"I'm sure you're right," Saracen said. "But I still need to ask the questions. After all, your gran invited Daphne here."

Gran's eyes narrowed. "Because Daphne was a friend. I wanted her at my wedding to celebrate my marriage to Ray. I didn't invite her here to thump her over the head with a bottle."

"How do you know about the bottle?" Saracen's gaze cut to me and he frowned.

I winced. "Sorry, but there was no point in hiding it from her. Gran's no killer."

Saracen lifted a hand. "This need not be complicated, but if I don't ask the questions, the police will."

"You're fine," Gran said. "Come take a seat. I'll answer any questions you have, and I'll show you I had nothing to do with what happened to Daphne."

"And I'm staying while you ask those questions," I said.

Saracen gave me a half smile. "I figured you would. I've got no problem with that." He perched on the edge of a kitchen chair. "I'll make this quick. It's looking likely that Daphne's death was no accident. I need to know where you were between the hours of nine-thirty and ten yesterday evening."

"At my wedding reception," Gran said. "There are plenty of witnesses. I was the woman dressed up, looking radiant as the new bride."

I glanced at her. She had been at the reception most of the time, but she did leave to change her shoes around that time, and had asked me to cover for her. I shook my head. That meant nothing. I trusted my gran.

"What relationship did you have with the victim?" Saracen said.

Gran lifted her chin. "Her name was Daphne, and I had a good relationship with her."

"And how did you know each other?"

She tutted. "I suspect you know the answer to that question."

"Even so, I'd like to hear you tell me."

"We met while we were serving time in prison."

Saracen glanced at me and cleared his throat. "About that. The police are interested in your criminal record."

"Once a criminal, always a criminal." Gran waved a hand in the air. "But if they bother to check my record, they won't see any violent crime in my past."

"What did you go to prison for?" Saracen said.

"Is that information necessary?" I said.

"I need to get a complete picture of all the suspects and their possible motives," Saracen said. "If you wouldn't mind answering the question, Molly."

"I don't mind. And you can find out the information easily enough if you bothered looking." Gran shrugged. "I took from the rich, and I gave to the poor."

"You being the poor?" Saracen said.

"It's not a crime to look after yourself," Gran said. "I was left in a difficult situation by an untrustworthy man and had to be resourceful. I never took anything from anyone who couldn't afford to lose it. I regret nothing I did."

"I expect you regret getting caught," Saracen said.

"Actually, I don't. I made a mistake, I got sloppy, and I paid the price. And I learned my lesson from it. I served my time, and while I was doing that, I made some amazing friends. Daphne was one of them."

"And you had no problems with Daphne?" Saracen said.

"No problems at all," Gran said.

He frowned. "So why do I have witnesses telling me they heard you arguing with Daphne at the reception?"

"They're lying!" I said. "There was no argument."

"I have reports stating you weren't happy with Daphne's outfit," Saracen said. "You had a disagreement about it."

"That was nothing," I said. "And I was there when it happened. It was more of a friendly chat. They weren't fighting over a dress. No one kills over a dress!"

"This is ridiculous," Gran said. "You're right, I wasn't happy Daphne bought an almost identical outfit to me, but I wasn't surprised."

"You admit you were rivals?" Saracen said.

"Not rivals. It was healthy competition," Gran said. "There's no harm in that."

"And I don't expect you were happy when Daphne flirted with Ray," Saracen said.

"This is getting ridiculous," I said. "Daphne made a few flirty comments when she was right in front of Gran. She didn't mean anything by them."

"You heard the comments?" Saracen said.

"Yes, and I wasn't concerned about them. It was just fun."

"That was Daphne being Daphne," Gran said. "She was always like that. I was used to it."

"What about the prison records we have?" Saracen said.

"We've been over those," Gran said. "I served at the same time as Daphne, that's how we got to be friends, and that's why she was at my wedding."

He shifted in his seat. "I was referring to the incidents in prison. The fights."

Gran's face paled, and she slid a finger across her empty plate. "That was nothing. It was a long time ago."

My stomach tightened. It took a lot to shake Gran up, and Saracen's comment had done just that. "What fights?"

She glanced at me, a guilty look on her face. "When we first met, it took us a few weeks to get the pecking order right."

"Did you fight with Daphne while you were in prison?" I asked.

"There were one or two tiny incidents," Gran said. "Nothing bad. Sometimes, I had to use force to get people to respect me."

Saracen pulled out his phone and scrolled through it. "The warden has details that Daphne had a black eye and bruised ribs. And although she never reported it was you who attacked her, there's reason to believe you were involved."

I stifled a gasp behind my hand. Gran had attacked Daphne?

"Those reports were exaggerated. You should ask to see the report showing I lost a clump of hair and a tooth after Daphne went for me."

My mouth fell open. Who was this woman sitting in my kitchen?

Gran looked up at me, and shame filtered across her face. "I was a different person back then. I had to stand up for myself. I wasn't going to be pushed around by anyone or exploited. Daphne thought she could do that when we first met. I showed her otherwise. After we'd gone a few rounds, we became friends."

This wouldn't look good to the police. They'd see Gran as a criminal who'd previously injured Daphne, and now she was dead.

I touched Saracen's arm. "That was a long time ago. You know my gran. She's a kind person."

He nodded as he put away his phone. "Of course. But I'm making sure I cover everything the police will look into. They'll see this and think the worst."

I nodded. I didn't believe Gran was a killer, but her murky past wasn't doing her any favors.

"Is there anything else you can tell me about last night?" Saracen said. "Any other suspects I need to look at?"

Gran simply shook her head.

"Reggie!" I said. "Daphne's boyfriend. I don't trust him. I caught him on the phone, sweet talking someone. He got mean when he spotted me listening. Campbell was there, and he saw it happen."

"Reggie is a possibility," Gran said. "They were always arguing, and Daphne confided in me that she wanted done with him. The trouble was, she didn't want to go solo. She was worried no one else would want her, so she stuck with him. Better the devil you know, but he's got a violent past."

"We have him on the list to talk to," Saracen said. "You didn't see him slip out of the reception around the time of the murder, or see him fighting with Daphne that night?"

Gran shook her head. "Nothing like that."

"You really should look at Reggie," I said. "He's a scary guy. And he uses intimidation to get what he wants. What if Daphne stood up to him and he didn't like it?"

Saracen raised a hand. "I will speak to him."

"And stop looking into my gran," I said.

He sighed. "Holly, I have to do my job properly. I don't want the police to catch us out on anything. And with Campbell out of the picture, I can't mess this up."

"Where's Campbell?" Gran said.

"Oh, I meant to tell you. Campbell got arrested last night for punching a police officer when he stopped him from seeing Alice. Campbell's been suspended from duty."

Gran's mouth fell open. "That's bad. We need Campbell. He's not my favorite person, but he usually comes through."

"Saracen will help us. And sorry if I'm being snappy," I said to him. "I know you're doing everything you can. It's just ..." I waved a hand at Gran.

He nodded. "I get it."

"Thanks. I have to keep Gran safe."

"I'm fine. This isn't my first rumble with the law. Don't worry about me," she said.

Of course, I'd worry about her. She was family. "How's Alice doing?" I asked Saracen.

He shook his head. "She isn't doing so well. She had a restless night, and the doctor's been back this morning to sedate her again."

"That won't do her any good. Alice needs to know what she's saying and have a chance to get her thoughts in order. Drugging her will only make this harder."

"I hope to speak to her later. And the police have already been back. I've managed to put them off for now, but I can only do it for a few more hours," Saracen said. "They're demanding answers. Apparently, there's a new guy in charge, and he doesn't like the way things have been handled in the past."

That was the last thing we needed. Audley Castle always managed its problems privately and used the police as back-up if needed. We didn't want a new boss messing with things, especially not with Alice and Gran on the persons of interest list.

"I'm leading most of the inquiries, but the police could come sniffing around this way," Saracen said. "That's why I wanted to check with you, Molly, make sure you had everything clear in your mind."

"I'll only tell them the same thing I told you," Gran said. "Daphne was a friend, and I was at the reception with everyone else when she was attacked. I know nothing else that can help you."

"I'm sure we'll figure this out." Saracen stood. "I appreciate you taking the time to fill me in. I'll leave you to it."

My phone buzzed, and I pulled it out of my pocket. "Hi, Rupert. Can I call you back? Now's not a good time."

"Are you on your way?"

"On my way to where?"

"Breakfast with my parents. We're waiting for you."

I sucked in a breath. I'd forgotten all about it. "I'll be ten minutes."

"You'd better hurry. They don't like to be kept waiting."

I ended the call and shoved my phone away. My hair was damp, I had no make-up on, and I'd thrown on jeans and a sweater with a dog's face on the front. This wasn't a great second impression to make.

I looked over at Gran. Why hadn't she told the truth about leaving the reception last night? What was the point of lying about that?

I glanced at Saracen, who was studying the notes on his phone again. Gran was concealing something, and I needed to know why, but I couldn't ask her in front of Saracen.

This was a mystery to figure out later. First, I had a breakfast date to get through.

Chapter 8

"Gran, I've got to go. I'm late for breakfast with Rupert's parents."

She waved me away. "You go. I'll be fine. I've got plenty of wedding cake to keep me happy, and Ray will be back soon."

Saracen looked longingly at the cake.

"You're sure you'll be okay without me?" I asked.

"I'll be fine. You need to think about your future happiness, not worry about your silly old Gran. Go and impress Rupert's parents. I bet they can't wait to have you as a daughter-in-law."

I grimaced. I doubted that from the frosty reception I got last night. "I'll come with you, Saracen, if you're going back to the castle."

"Sure. That's where I'm heading."

I kissed Gran goodbye, then we left. I attempted to smooth my hair and get it to dry as I raced along with Meatball bouncing beside me.

"What's the hurry?" Saracen said.

"There was an unexpected arrival at the castle last night. Rupert and Alice's parents are here."

"I think I've only met them once. They rarely come to stay here. Are they visiting because of Alice?"

"No, they had no idea about the murder until after they arrived," I said. "They're here to meet me."

He slowed and stared at me before a smile spread across his face. "Of course. They want to check out the woman Lord Rupert's fallen for."

I smacked his arm as he chuckled. "This is no joke. Our first meeting last night wasn't a success. I've got work to do if I'm going to get them to like me."

"Bake them one of your cakes, that always wins people over."

"That's not a bad idea. I could make them a special cake. Thanks, Saracen."

"You can always bake me something nice, too."

"I always do." He was my willing guinea pig when it came to creating low sugar treats he could eat so as not to upset his diabetes.

"Be your usual self," he said. "Although maybe don't poke around in their business as much as you do everyone else's. They may not like that."

"Thanks for the tip. I wish I'd had time to get changed, though."

"Why? Your dog sweater is cute."

"It'll have to do."

"You'll wow them. You've got nothing to worry about. The only person you really need to be worried about impressing is Lord Rupert, and you've done that. He's been mooning around ever since you started working here. The guy is crazy about you. It took him long enough to make his move though."

I grinned, my cheeks growing warm. "There's nothing wrong with a slow burn relationship. But I'm struggling to focus on Rupert or his parents right now. You need to tell me everything you know about Daphne's murder, so we can get Alice and my gran off the hook quickly."

Saracen's mouth twisted to the side. "I don't know about that. You know two of the suspects. Is it a good idea you get involved?"

"A hundred percent yes! It's Alice and Gran. I have to make sure neither of them gets charged with murder."

He nodded. "You could be useful. I know you can get anyone to talk when you provide enough cake."

"I will, you can guarantee it. And I promise you an endless supply of sugar-free treats if you keep me in the loop."

Saracen grinned. "Sure. Let's work on this together. What do you want to know first?"

"Alice. We need to start with her. After all, she was found with the victim."

"Yes, that's tricky to get around. Princess Alice is an obvious suspect, given the situation."

"You know she didn't do it. You have to get the police to see she was an innocent bystander who got mixed up in something she can't remember."

"That's a problem we're trying to figure out. What caused her memory loss? There are no signs of injury on her body, so she didn't get a blow to the head that affected her short-term memory, but she's adamant she doesn't remember how she got into that room."

"Check with her doctor. He drew blood samples last night. He could use that to see if there was anything in her system that affected her memory."

"I'll get on that right away," Saracen said. "Do you think she was drugged?"

"It's one possible explanation. And if she was, then someone gave it to her. And that someone must be the killer."

Saracen nodded. "Then, as you know, your gran's also a suspect."

"Which I completely disagree with," I said.

"You've got to admit, with her dodgy background and criminal past—"

"A criminal past with no record of violence."

"Her prison record suggests otherwise," Saracen said.

I chewed on my bottom lip. I was still surprised by that revelation. "That was an extreme circumstance. She had to show she wasn't a pushover. It doesn't mean she's usually violent. Although ..."

"Something's worrying you about your gran?"

"I'll admit, I had no idea Gran and Daphne didn't get along when they met, but they must have sorted it out, or Gran wouldn't have invited her to the wedding. And she wouldn't want to kill anyone on her wedding day. You don't want to be stuck with that memory. Happy wedding anniversary and happy-I-murdered-my-best-friend anniversary. It doesn't fit."

"It doesn't when you put it like that, but there was violence between them, and your gran and Daphne were heard arguing."

"Not arguing, having a heated chat because Daphne bought the same outfit as my gran. They've always been competitive, and it's never led to murder."

"Weddings are stressful. Maybe your gran snapped."

I held up a hand. "Don't even go there. It wasn't her." I was considering telling Saracen that Gran had snuck out of the reception around the time of the murder, but it wouldn't help her if I revealed that fact. And it wasn't relevant. She'd simply gone out to get a change of shoes and had nothing to do with what happened to Daphne.

"If it's any consolation, I've gotten to know your gran since she moved to Audley St. Mary, and I like her. She's feisty, but I've never seen her as dangerous. I'll do my best to convince the police to look elsewhere."

"They need to look hard at Daphne's date, Reggie Frasier. He's shady. I didn't feel safe around him."

"You've got that right about him being shady," Saracen said. "The guy wouldn't know how to walk a straight line if there was one painted in bright neon in front of him."

"There you go! Gran said Daphne was unhappy with Reggie. And I caught him snooping around the castle."

"What was he snooping for?"

"I spoke to Campbell about this. I think Reggie was looking to steal some family silver. He was taking pictures on his phone and then sending messages. And don't forget, I caught him talking to another woman. He was supposed to be Daphne's boyfriend. What if she caught him messing around with someone else? She could have confronted him last night, and he had to silence her."

"It's a motive," Saracen said. "And Reggie has strong ties to the mob."

"I heard that about him too. What work did he do for them?"

"He was an enforcer. If someone had a debt to pay or a problem with any member in the mob, Reggie was sent to remind them of their place."

"You mean he beat them until they were so terrified they wouldn't cause trouble for the mob again?"

"Yeah, that's pretty much it."

"Isn't he a bit old to go around thumping people?" I said.

"He has more of a background role these days, but once you're in that kind of group, you never leave. They always keep tabs on you to make sure you're not shouting your mouth off about your criminal associations."

"And just because he's a bit long in the tooth to beat someone up, it doesn't mean he's stopped throwing his weight around with women," I said.

Saracen scowled. "I can't stand a guy who uses his fists on a woman. Do you know if Daphne ever mentioned that Reggie got physical with her?"

"No, but I'll check with Gran and Daphne's other friends. I reckon Daphne could hold her own if Reggie went for her, but maybe things got out of hand last night."

"Did you see Reggie at the reception when Daphne was in trouble?"

"I was watching him closely, but I can't remember where he was at the time Daphne was killed."

"I'll make sure to question Reggie before he leaves. Even if it's just to rule him out."

"Don't rule him out. It has to be him. It can't be Alice or Gran."

"I don't disagree with you, but right now, Princess Alice and your gran are the top suspects in the police's eyes."

"Maybe they are, but I'll do my own follow-up with Reggie to make sure nothing gets missed."

"Holly, be careful around Reggie. Guys like him have no morals or boundaries. If you get in his way, he'll crush you. And if he thinks you're trying to pin this murder on him, he will silence you."

I pretended not to notice the fear welling up inside me. I'd do whatever it took to keep Gran and Alice safe.

Saracen gave my elbow a quick squeeze. "I know I can't keep you out of this, but don't put yourself at risk."

Saracen knew me too well. "I will ask questions. I need to get Alice and Gran in the clear. And I know you want to do the same, but you have the police looking at what you're doing. I don't. That means I can sneak around and find out more."

Saracen ran a hand over his close-cropped hair. "Just be careful. This is my first time in charge, and I don't want anyone to get hurt."

"You're doing a great job so far."

"Sure I am. Keep me informed about what you find out. I have plenty of resources at my disposal if you need them. You don't have to do this on your own."

"I will. And you do the same for me. Campbell does when he thinks I can be helpful, even though the information is sometimes grudgingly given."

Saracen grinned. "You can bet it is. The first time you wore him down enough so you could be involved in a case, he didn't stop complaining about you for days."

"I can imagine. I bet he now sees me as an indispensable asset."

Saracen's grin faded. "Something like that. I'd much prefer it if he was in charge."

"How's he doing?" I said. "I saw him last night trying to get to Princess Alice."

"Not so good. I was shocked when the Duchess informed me Campbell was no longer a part of the team. She only gave me the basic details, but when I saw Betsy cleaning this morning, she filled me in. He keeps messaging me and asking how things are going."

"He must be so worried about Alice. We all know he's been desperately in love with her for as long as I can remember, even though he denies it. It must be killing him that he can't help her when she needs it the most."

Saracen chuckled. "We all know that. And you're right, he's out of the loop and powerless. It's the worst position to be in."

We reached the castle, and I turned to Saracen. "I'll let you know as soon as I hear anything useful."

"And I'll do the same for you. Good luck, Holly." Saracen hurried away.

I pulled back my shoulders and looked at the imposing entrance to the castle. I needed to focus on my immediate crisis. First, I had to charm my future in-laws, then I'd question Reggie and get the truth out of him about his relationship with Daphne.

Chapter 9

It was only when I was walking toward the closed dining-room door that my knees shook. This breakfast meeting with Rupert's parents was a huge deal, and I wasn't prepared. I should have answers ready for the numerous questions they were bound to ask me.

Although I was surprised we were still having breakfast at all, given the serious situation Alice was in. Rupert must have told them everything that was going on, but since the breakfast was going ahead, I had to believe they had everything in hand.

Perhaps their lawyer was amazing and always solved their problems. Although I doubted they'd ever faced a problem as large as one of their children being accused of murder!

I stopped by the door with Meatball and stared at it. If this was going to be my future home, should I knock, or act like I already belonged to the family?

Meatball nudged my leg with his head and sniffed the bottom of the door.

"I know, we should just go in. They're not that intimidating." My hand went to the door knob, then I stepped back. I should knock. I wasn't a part of the family yet and didn't want to look arrogant and assume a role before I'd even accepted Rupert's marriage proposal.

I grinned. Rupert wanted to marry me. I got that funny butterfly feeling in my stomach every time I remembered that.

I sucked in a deep breath and was just about to knock, when the door was opened. Rupert stood on the other side.

His warm smile immediately reassured me. "There you are. Is everything okay?" He leaned forward and kissed my cheek.

"Everything's good. I'm sorry we're late. What with everything going on ..." I gestured around, trying to encompass the chaos without mentioning murder suspects, the police, and wedding shambles.

"You're fine." Although Rupert's smile was still warm, there was worry in his eyes. "But we'd better get in. Father hates cold food."

I tugged his hand before we entered the room. "How much do they know about what happened last night?"

"I told them everything about the murder and Alice being in the room."

My eyebrows rose. "And how are they taking it?"

"The usual stiff upper lip. Let's have breakfast and you can find out more."

I walked into the grand dining room with its solid oak paneling on the walls, a huge fireplace dominating one wall, and a long table containing breakfast.

Lord Audley sat at the head of the table, and his wife sat to his right.

Rupert pulled out a chair for me, and I sat down.

"Sorry I'm late. I had a family emergency."

Lady Audley nodded at me. "You're here now." Her gaze shifted to Meatball.

"Is it okay he's in here? He's always very good."

"He may stay." She cut off a small piece of toast and threw it to him.

Rupert poured me a cup of coffee and nodded at me encouragingly.

I swallowed. Was I supposed to start the conversation?

Lady Audley dabbed her napkin against her lips and then set it down. "So, Holly. Rupert has been telling us all about you. You read history at university?"

"That's right," I said.

"You didn't pursue it as a career choice?"

"No, I was struggling to find work in that field after I graduated. My second love has always been baking. I took courses at college and even ran my own café for a while in the village."

"That failed as a business, I believe." Rupert's dad didn't look at me as he perused the morning paper.

"Oh, well, it was successful for almost a year, but then a chain café moved into the village and undercut my prices. I struggled on for a bit but couldn't cover all the bills. I had no choice but to close. I was looking around after the business ended, wondering what to do next, when I saw the position at Audley Castle."

"And it was a perfect fit for Holly," Rupert said. "She loves history, so gets to spend all her time looking at this crumbling old place while she makes the most delicious desserts you'll ever taste. We're lucky to have found her. I'm amazed she hasn't been scooped up by some Michelin starred chef ages ago."

I smiled at him. He always loved singing my praises.

"We have heard good things about your food," Lady Audley said. "But I'm curious about your prospects. Do you plan to continue working in the kitchen if this marriage to Rupert goes ahead?"

"When it goes ahead," Rupert said.

I raised my eyebrows at him. I hadn't formally accepted a proposal. "I love to bake. And I like earning my own money."

"You won't need to earn money when you're a part of this family," Lord Audley said. "I suppose that's why you're interested in this whole business."

"Father! Holly's not like that. I spent a long time trying to get her interested in me. She's far too good for me, and I never thought she'd agree to even date me." Rupert's cheeks flushed pink. "Sorry, Holly."

Lord Audley glanced at me before returning his attention to the paper beside him without making any further comment.

"It does happen though," Lady Audley murmured. "You read about it in the magazines. Women chasing men for their fortunes."

"Not with us," Rupert said.

I nodded, biting my tongue in case I said something rude after being called a gold digger.

"Holly, I understand you like to bake, but there will be expectations of you if you take a role in this family," Lady Audley said. "My husband and I spend many months of the year traveling. We're involved in prestigious committees and events and do our bit for charity. You won't have time to hold down a full-time job and do all that."

I blinked at Rupert. "Is that what you want us to do?"

He set down his knife and fork. "It's not something we've discussed, and I'm not pushing you into anything, but it would be nice to be more community minded. I was thinking we could support local charities. The castle is perfect for fundraising events, and the kitchen could provide the food. I don't just want to do the social side of the charity work, then give a donation at the end of the night. If we're going to be philanthropists, I want to be hands-on." Rupert turned to his mother. "And Holly's passionate about animal welfare. There's a wonderful local rescue in need of a patron. That could be ideal as our first project."

"I didn't know they needed a patron," I said.

He smiled at me. "I've been doing research, seeing what charities we may like to support. Of course, you get to pick along with me."

"It would be wonderful to support the local rescue center," I said. "And I'm all on board for being hands-on. I don't just want to give them the money and run."

"Are you suggesting that's what we do?" Lady Audley said.

"Oh, no! But you sound busy. I'm sure you'd like to do more." I took a sip of my coffee so I had a few seconds to gather my thoughts. So far, this wasn't going well, but at least I hadn't thrown anything at Lord Audley for being rude about my romantic interest in Rupert.

"What about managing the new estate your father is considering?" Lady Audley said to Rupert. "We've found several interesting locations in Italy. There's also the possibility of a place in Dubai."

"Dubai's too hot," I said. "And I don't want to travel all that way with Meatball. He likes it around here."

"Your fondness for animals is admirable," Lady Audley said. "But there are excellent kennels you can use. Perhaps he could stay here, or you can get him a passport so he can travel with you."

"I'm not all that keen on long-distance travel either," Rupert said.

"So I've noticed," Lady Audley said. "You've turned down three invitations to spend the summer with us. Anyone would think you didn't like your parents."

Rupert glanced at me and his cheeks flushed. "I've been busy here. I didn't want to spend months away from the castle or Holly."

Lady Audley sipped her fruit juice. "And what about children?"

My eyes widened, while Rupert looked on helplessly. "What about them?"

"Do you want them?"

"I, um, eventually. Maybe. I love looking after Meatball. I always call him my fur baby."

"Having children is not the same as looking after an animal," Lady Audley said. "And we have to ensure the continuation of our family line."

"I'm happy to talk about children with Rupert, but that's a conversation to have in private," I said.

Rupert nodded. "Absolutely. Mother, you're forgetting, Holly and I are only dating."

"But you do see marriage in your future," Lady Audley said. "Therefore, it's important you know what your ambitions are when it comes to children. You don't want to be married, and then five years down the line one of you changes your mind, or reveals you never wanted children. That would end in heartache. When I agreed to marry your father, we talked about all these things. My future work, the number of children we wanted, our travel intentions. It's important to lay the groundwork so there are no nasty surprises in the future."

"I agree. It's always good to plan which direction you're going," I said, "but there will always be surprises along the way. I don't expect you ever planned to find Alice in so much trouble."

"She's not in trouble," Lady Audley said.

I glanced at Rupert. "Oh! That's good news. Has she remembered what happened last night? Did she see who attacked Daphne?"

"No, but our lawyer is on the way. He'll sort this out."

"You must be worried about Alice, though. And she must be so scared."

"Alice is a silly girl, but she's not violent," Lord Audley said.

"I know that." Their continuing lack of concern was alarming. Was this how they always behaved when a family member was in trouble? "We've become good friends since I started working here."

"Yes, she often mentions you when we speak," Lady Audley said. "I thought she was joking when she said she was making friends with a kitchen assistant. How did that unusual friendship come about?"

Rupert cleared his throat. "Alice has an excellent choice in friends. She saw how kind and warm-hearted Holly was as soon as she started working here. We all did. So will you when you get to know her."

"Have you been to see Alice this morning?" I chose to ignore the less than subtle swipe Lady Audley had made at me.

"I had a brief look at her, but she was asleep," Lady Audley said. "The doctor's been by and settled her. Once Peterson has done what he needs to, this business can be forgotten about."

"Perhaps I should go see her," I said.

"No, stay here," Lady Audley said. "Alice needs complete rest."

I wiped my clammy hands on my jeans. I didn't want to stay another moment. I wanted to be with Alice and make sure she wasn't freaking out, especially considering the blasé way her parents were treating her situation as a murder suspect.

"Holly could take five minutes to see Alice," Rupert said.

"I would prefer it if she remains here," Lady Audley said. "I have more questions. It's important we're all comfortable if this match happens."

I braced myself for the next round of questions, but tilted my head at the sound of a car pulling up outside. I glanced out the window and my stomach tightened. It was a police car, and Campbell was standing next to it. They must have let him go.

I pushed my seat back. "If you'll excuse me, I just need to—"

"Remain here," Lady Audley said. "Anyone would think you don't want to get to know us. Don't you want to be a part of this family?"

I stared at her in disbelief. I cared deeply for Rupert, but why couldn't she see her other child needed help, and I could be the one to offer that?

"Now, where was I?" Lady Audley sipped her fruit juice again. "Oh, yes, children. What are your thoughts on boarding school?"

I looked at Rupert for help.

"Mother, it's too soon to talk about children and their education," he said.

"I like the Mistelthorpes," Lord Audley said.

"What was that, my dear?" A flash of irritation crossed Lady Audley's face.

"Holly's family. The Mistelthorpes. That's who she's connected to, isn't that right?"

"I believe so, although it's a distant connection," Lady Audley said. "She wasn't raised by them."

"It's still valid," Rupert said. "And her relatives are decent people. They've kept in touch regularly ever since Holly learned of her connection to them."

"Yes, they have. Now, if you don't mind, I—"

"Your connection is useful," Lady Audley said. "But what about your immediate family? The people who raised you. Tell me about them."

I looked at the police car. Two officers stood beside it, talking to Campbell. "I, um, I don't have much immediate family. I have a step-mother and a sister, and my gran."

"Your gran. Tell me about her. What's her background?"

There was no way I was disclosing a single thing about Gran. If Lord and Lady Audley got wind she was also involved in this murder and a reformed prisoner, that would be another nail in the coffin for me and Rupert.

"I don't see this match being a problem," Lord Audley said. "If the Mistelthorpes vouch for Holly, I'll respect their opinion."

I forced myself not to gape at him. He respected their opinion but had barely paid me any attention. I squeezed my hands into fists. I could only bite my tongue for so long.

"I'm playing golf with Alistair Mistelthorpe tomorrow. We can talk about Holly, make sure everything is above board. Check out the prospects, that kind of thing."

I gritted my teeth. "I assure you, my prospects are excellent."

"That's right," Rupert said. "I'm lucky Holly is even considering marrying me. And I don't care if she's connected to the Queen of England or a local chimney sweep, she makes me happy."

"We need to cover the bases," his dad said. "If Holly passes muster with the Mistelthorpes, we can move on to something more interesting."

My breathing grew shallow. Not only was I not worth speaking to, I was also uninteresting.

Lady Audley sighed. "I suppose if that's the way you want to do it. And once Holly has changed her name to Audley, we can smooth over her background and forge a strong alliance with the Mistelthorpes."

I pushed my chair back with a loud squeak and stood. "I may not want to change my surname. I'm proud of being a Holmes. My dad was a great man, and I loved him very much. My gran's a wonderful woman too. She's caring, loving, and generous. And just because I don't have some regal background, it doesn't mean I'm not worthy of being with Rupert. Now, if you'll excuse me, I need to be somewhere else."

"You can't leave," Lady Audley said. "We have matters to discuss. Your future with my son is important."

"Mother, that's enough interrogation. Holly's right, she can be an Audley, a Holmes, a Mistelthorpe, or any other name she chooses. Whatever makes her happy."

"I've never heard of anything so preposterous," Lady Audley said. "Names matter."

I nodded at the window. "Rupert, I need to get out there."

"You go. I'll stay here. You see what's going on."

I dashed out of the dining room with Meatball, not waiting to hear the curt chastisements coming out of Lady Audley's mouth. Was I making a huge mistake getting involved in this family? Rupert had stood up for me during question time, but this was too much. His parents had no right to plan out our future without consulting us, or even speaking to me.

I shook my head. I couldn't worry about them. Some things were more important than keeping my future in-laws happy.

I had to hope that was right, and I hadn't just made a huge mistake, one I'd live to regret.

It was too late now, the damage was done. And I was needed elsewhere. Alice and Gran needed me to keep them safe.

Chapter 10

I raced out the doors of the castle and onto the gravel driveway with Meatball. Campbell was still talking to the two police officers. I vaguely recognized them, which was good. It hopefully meant they wouldn't be too stubborn with Campbell, and they may even be on our side.

"Hey, Campbell, what's going on?" I said. "Are you in trouble over last night?"

He turned, fury in his eyes as his hands fisted by his sides. "Last night was nothing. I'm trying to stop them from taking Alice. They want to arrest her for Daphne's murder."

I gasped and stared at the police. "You have the wrong person."

"We're not arresting her," the short, male officer said. "Not yet."

"You can't do that," I said. "Alice has done nothing wrong."

"We have our orders," the tall, female police officer with short dark hair said. "We need to take her in for questioning and get a statement. No charges have been decided upon at this stage."

"It's only a matter of time before they are," Campbell muttered.

"What evidence have you got against Alice?" I said.

"We can't talk about an ongoing case," the female police officer said.

Silent fury radiated off Campbell as he jerked his head to the side. I hurried away from the police car with him and out of earshot of the officers.

"What do you know?" I said to him.

"It's bad news," he said.

"Campbell!" Saracen strode over. "I got here as soon as I heard you were back. They didn't tell me they were coming to take Princess Alice."

"The police aren't planning on keeping us in the loop anymore," Campbell said. "There's a new guy in charge, and he's brought in some of his old team. They don't know how things work around here, and that's making it difficult to get information, or make any of them see sense."

"I still don't understand why they're here for Alice," I said. "Nothing's changed overnight, has it?"

"It has, and not in a good way. Alice woke up a little while ago," Saracen said. "And she as good as confessed to killing Daphne."

My stomach dropped, and I clutched it tight, the tiny amount of breakfast I'd eaten threatening to come back up. "Why would she do that? When I spoke to her, she had no memory of how she got in that room, never mind killing Daphne."

"The police claim she said she did it." Campbell snorted. "They're twisting her words, they have to be. They can't get past the fact she was found in that room, clutching what was most likely the murder weapon."

"What about the blood samples the doctor took from Alice? That must show something strange. She was drugged, that was why she passed out," I said.

"We're still waiting on those results," Saracen said.

"That doctor needs to get a move on." Campbell practically growled out the words.

"There's another problem," Saracen said. "The police are worried about Alice's mental stability."

"There's nothing wrong with her mental health," I said. "She's eccentric, but then the whole family are. What are they going to do, blame them for crimes simply because they're odd?"

"They're making a case. Apparently, one of Princess Alice's great aunts was sectioned for most of her life," Saracen said.

"That's meaningless to this investigation," Campbell said.

"Not to the police."

"What was she sectioned for?" I said.

"The great aunt started having delusions when she was in her mid-twenties. At first, people didn't pay it much attention. Then she was found wandering around the grounds of her home naked. It became a regular occurrence, and she started telling anyone who'd listen that the voices in her head were telling her to do that. Some of her delusions became dark, and she injured a member of her staff.

After that, she had a short stay in the sanatorium. That led to longer stays, courses of different drugs, and she finally died," Saracen said.

"I mean, that's terrible," I said, "but it has nothing to do with Alice. She's healthy."

"She is," Campbell muttered. "There's nothing wrong with her."

"It gets worse. They're also looking at Lady Philippa's mental health," Saracen said. "They think there's a family history of mental ill health, and it's been passed on to Princess Alice."

Campbell groaned and his chin dropped to his chest. "Don't tell me she's been talking about her visions again?"

"Campbell, you were there last night. How would Lady Philippa have known anything was wrong with Alice or Daphne if she didn't have some kind of pre-cognitive ability?"

"Be quiet," he hissed. "Don't say anything like that when the police are around. It'll only make things worse for Princess Alice."

"I won't. But we all know there's something special about Lady Philippa. I'm not saying Alice inherited that ability, but it's possible. And maybe this great aunt had the same ability, but she was labeled crazy because of it."

"That's no help to us," Campbell said. "And Lady Philippa's eccentricities are a problem if that's the angle the police are going for. I've seen the notebooks in her room. She writes down these ridiculous visions and dreams. If the police have gotten wind of that, put the crazy great aunt and Lady Philippa's problems together, and then look at Alice and her memory loss, and the case is solved. Princess Alice lost her mind and got a voice or a vision telling her to hit Daphne." He turned away, his body shaking with anger. "It's what I'd think if it was anyone but Princess Alice."

I turned and peered through the dining room windows where Rupert and Alice's parents still sat. "Is that what Lord and Lady Audley think about Alice?"

"Why do you ask?" Campbell turned back. "Have they said something?"

"It's more what they haven't said that's bothering me. If my daughter was up on a murder charge, I'd be frantic with worry. But they're not bothered and think it'll blow over. I just had breakfast with them, and they seemed unconcerned about her well-being. They just keep saying everything will be cleared up when the lawyer gets here."

"What's your point, Holly?" Campbell said.

"What if they're behind this mental instability angle? They've suggested Alice is unwell to the police and therefore not responsible for her actions. They think she killed Daphne and plan to get her off by claiming insanity."

Campbell stared at me, his expression tightening.

"Let's not get ahead of ourselves. I haven't spoken to Lord and Lady Audley this morning," Saracen said. "But they didn't mention anything last night about an insanity plea."

"I wouldn't waste your time going after them to find out more," I said. "Alice was dismissed as a silly child when I questioned them, but maybe this is why they're not concerned. They're making arrangements with the police and their lawyer. They think Alice is going the same way as her great aunt."

"They've never thought much of Princess Alice," Campbell said. "They've never treated her well. She gets all the material things she likes, but not much love. I think she wishes the Duke and Duchess were her real parents."

My heart went out to Alice. I really wanted to see her and reassure her everything would be okay. I also wanted to make sure she stopped talking, just in case she let slip she'd had a vision last night, or something unexplainable had happened that led her to seek out Daphne. It wouldn't do her any favors, particularly if this lawyer and her parents were going after an insanity plea.

"I should go speak to the police," Saracen said.

"You do that," Campbell said. "Let us know what they tell you."

Saracen nodded at him and then hurried away.

"Holly, I have a solution to our problem," Campbell said. "I wasn't sure about doing it, but now I know her parents aren't supporting her, it has to happen."

"You know how to show Alice and my gran are innocent?"

"I can't do anything about your gran. I'm sorry she's involved in this, but I'm focused on protecting Princess Alice. You must understand that."

"What are you thinking?"

"The police are moments away from taking in Princess Alice. She's vulnerable and likely to say something she'll regret. I have to make sure that doesn't happen."

"I don't disagree, but what can you do?"

"I need you to cover for me. I'm getting out of here, and I'm taking Princess Alice with me."

My jaw dropped. "You can't! If Alice runs, it'll make her look guilty."

"And if she stays, she'll get even more entangled in this mess and we won't be able to get her out. Once the police start their interrogation, she's done for, especially if she thinks she's guilty." Campbell gripped my arm. "Holly, you saw the scene last night. She was next to the victim, she had the murder weapon in her hand, and she was covered in blood. If I didn't know Alice, I'd say she was guilty. I'd be hauling her in for questioning and trying to break through her lies."

I tipped back my head and stared at the sky. "The lawyer's on his way. He could help clear her name. And there's still the doctor's report to come back. If that shows Alice has drugs in her system, then we'll know she's innocent."

"No, I think you have the right idea. This lawyer will press the idea of mental instability and get her off on a technicality. It'll still make her look guilty, and it'll still mean she has to spend time in a secure unit being treated for a condition she doesn't have. And as for the drugs supposedly in her system, we've got no proof they're there. What if the doctor's report comes back, and it's clear? Then we've gotten nowhere and wasted time. It'll be too late for Princess Alice."

I looked at the police as they talked to Saracen. We really were running out of time.

Campbell squeezed my elbow. "You have to help me, especially if Princess Alice is talking about being guilty. If she's not sure what happened, she may think she was involved. I can't have her saying the wrong thing."

"Campbell, I don't know. How are you going to get her out of the castle without being spotted?"

"I've got an idea, but I need you to cause a distraction, and take the police officers' attention away from me while I get inside and move Alice."

"What kind of distraction?"

Meatball gave a loud bark.

I looked down to see his attention was focused on the castle doors. A few seconds later, the Duchess emerged with her corgis, most of them already off their leashes.

"That'll work," Campbell said. "Meatball, go cause chaos with those stuck up furry snobs."

Meatball bounced on his paws and took a few steps toward the corgis. Several of them spotted him and started barking.

Meatball growled and his hackles rose.

"Campbell, I don't know about this," I said. "Are you sure you should take Alice?"

"Yes. I'm getting her away. We can prove she's innocent when she's out of danger. I need you to back me on this."

Meatball was still growling, slowly stalking toward the Duchess's corgis.

The desperation in Campbell's eyes made my heart ache. "Okay, I'll cover for you, but hurry."

He nodded, then dashed away.

I knelt next to Meatball and ruffled his fur. "I don't usually approve of you causing trouble, but our friend needs us. How about you roughhouse some of those corgis and show them who's boss around here?"

As if he understood me, Meatball's ears lowered a fraction, then he raced toward the Duchess and her corgis. At the last second, he veered to the left, and ran back to the police officers.

The Duchess's corgis saw the challenge and chased after him, yapping and growling.

I looked on as the police officers stopped talking to Saracen and stared at the oncoming stampede of small barking dogs.

"Boys, girls, come back! Oh, they're so feisty, they never listen to my commands," the Duchess said.

The corgis ignored her as they raced after their target. Meatball was way out in front. He wasn't overweight like most of the corgis, so could keep a healthy distance from them and not risk getting nipped.

"Officers! Stop those dogs," the Duchess called out.

The distraction couldn't have been more perfect. The police officers scattered, lunging at the corgis to try to catch them.

Meatball dodged the officers, raced around their car, then headed back toward them, the corgis in hot pursuit.

One of the officers held a squirming corgi in his arms, but he wriggled free and joined in the games again.

I looked back at the castle, trying to spot Campbell. His plan had me worried. If Alice fled, she'd be in big trouble. I wasn't sure this was the right thing to do.

My gaze cut to the door, and I winced as I spotted Rupert and Alice's parents emerge.

Lady Audley stared at the chaos, a frown on her face. Her expression hardened as she stared at me. "What on earth is going on?"

Chapter 11

Angry yapping filled the air as the police officers continued to chase after the corgis.

Lord and Lady Audley walked over to the Duchess, disdain on their faces.

"Isn't that your little dog in the middle of this mess?" Lady Audley said to me.

"Meatball is protecting himself," I said.

The Duchess looked at me and nodded. "I'm so sorry, Holly. I didn't realize he was out here. I know my lot like to chase him. They've never been able to get on."

"He's not a purebred," Lord Audley said. "They probably sense the difference."

"He may not be pure, but he's still perfect," I said.

Lord Audley simply nodded and shifted his gaze to the horizon.

"Oh, officer, bring that one over to me. I'll put him on his leash," the Duchess called out.

The female police officer walked over with a wriggling corgi in her arms. "You better be careful. This one tried to bite me."

"They never do any damage with their little teeth," the Duchess said. "Hurry! Go get that one by your car."

The officer looked like she was about to protest, but then shrugged and dashed off after the gallivanting dog.

"What are the police even doing here?" Lady Audley said.

"They're here for Alice," I said. "You didn't know they were coming?"

"Oh! I thought that business was being sorted out."

Saracen walked over. "If I may interrupt, there's been a development in the murder investigation. The police are here to take Princess Alice in for questioning."

Lord Audley's nostrils flared. "Take her in for questioning? That's not the plan. Here, look. That's Peterson's car coming along the driveway. He'll take care of everything. Alice won't need to go with the police."

I turned and spotted a sleek silver car gliding to a stop outside the castle. A tall, elegant man in his late-fifties emerged from the driver's seat. He straightened his red tie and then walked over to Lord Audley before shaking his hand.

"I'm glad you could get here so promptly," Lord Audley said. "I trust you're up to speed on the matter we discussed on the phone?"

Peterson nodded. "I contacted the police first thing. I'm not surprised to find them here."

"I suppose they have to be seen to be doing their jobs after a woman has died," Lord Audley said. "They'll back off now you're here to intervene."

"How are you intervening?" I said.

Peterson turned to me. "We've not met before."

"Holly Holmes," I said. "Alice's best friend. What are you going to do to prove her innocence?"

The lawyer shook my outstretched hand. "Percival Peterson. Nothing untoward will happen to Princess Alice."

"What do you mean by untoward? I've heard the police are worried about her mental health. You're not going to suggest she was ill and that led her to kill Daphne?"

Peterson glanced at Lord Audley, and I didn't miss him give a discreet shake of his head.

"This is a family matter to be decided upon," Lord Audley said.

"I'm almost family," I said.

"Not yet you're not," Lady Audley said. "Rupert told me you haven't accepted his proposal."

I gritted my teeth. "I'm still very close to Alice, and need to make sure she's safe. She won't want you suggesting she's mentally unwell in an attempt to get her off this murder charge. She's innocent."

Another look passed between Lord Audley and Peterson.

"We know what we're doing," Lord Audley said. "Alice will be fine, and maybe a short stay at a luxury spa is just what she needs. She must be stressed after discovering that woman's body."

Luxury spa my Aunt Fanny. They wanted to make out Alice had lost her mind, and she'd actually hurt Daphne. I wasn't letting them get away with this. I was glad I'd covered for Campbell. If this was the support Alice was getting from her family, the further away she was from them, the better.

"Rather than focusing on Alice, and assuming she's guilty, you need to look for other suspects," I said.

Peterson patted me on the shoulder. "I'm working closely with the police and am aware of all other persons of interest."

"Do you know about Reggie Frasier? He was the victim's boyfriend, and they weren't happy together. Daphne was even thinking about ending things with him. What if she'd done that last night? They could have argued and Reggie hit her."

Peterson shook his head. "As I said, I'm working with the police, and they're cooperating. I have the information I need to resolve this matter. Let's not go complicating things."

"Ignoring a prime suspect isn't a complication, it's illogical. Speak to Reggie."

The two police officers walked back with more corgis, and the Duchess quickly gathered them up, attaching their leashes.

"Thank you so much, officers," she said. "Holly, may I have a word with you about Meatball?"

"Good idea," Lady Audley said. "He's a cute little thing, but he's clearly a troublemaker." She glanced at me.

She didn't have to say it. It was clear from her expression that Lady Audley also considered me an unwanted trouble.

I picked up Meatball and walked away with the Duchess and her corgis. "Is Meatball in the doghouse? He didn't mean any harm."

She didn't speak until we were out of earshot of everyone else. "Of course not. I know my pack are ruffians. I've overindulged them over the years and this was all my fault. Meatball is a good boy." She petted him on the head as she leaned closer. "I'm not happy with what's happening to Alice. She's confused, and no one is telling her the truth about what's about to happen. The last thing I want is for her to be taken away."

Relief coursed through me. At last, Alice had someone else fighting her corner. "Have you seen her this morning?"

"I went in first thing. She's concerned she hurt that woman."

"You don't believe that, do you?"

"I don't. But the way things are going, Alice looks guilty. And having heard what the lawyer is proposing, her parents don't seem convinced of her innocence either."

"They want to sweep this under the carpet, don't they?"

She lifted one shoulder. "They're my family, just like Alice, so I won't speak badly of them, but they don't always have their children's best interests at heart. They're in favor of ensuring the family name isn't sullied by a scandal."

"Aren't they worried it'll be sullied if people think Alice has lost her mind?"

"You know these old families. I certainly do, having been a part of one for such a long time."

"You've lost me."

The Duchess arched an eyebrow. "There are always first and second cousins marrying each other. It sometimes doesn't end well. It's expected that the inbreeding will create instability. But I know Alice, and there's nothing wrong with her. She's a sweet young woman and doesn't deserve this."

"I agree." I looked at the castle. Should I tell her what Campbell had done? No, I couldn't expect the Duchess to keep that secret. "Is there anything you can do to help Alice?"

"I'll keep a close eye on the situation and try to make sure things don't go too far. I don't want her sent away and treated like a criminal, even if it is to a luxury spa." She patted my arm. "I just wanted you to know that I'm looking out for her."

"Alice will appreciate that. I know I do."

She nodded at me before walking off with her dogs.

I turned back to the rest of the group. Rupert had joined his parents, and they were all standing with Saracen. The police were nowhere to be seen.

I walked back to them. I wanted to tell Rupert what was going on with Alice, but I needed to do it when we were in private.

"I'll need to leave soon," Lord Audley said. "I can't be late for my meeting."

I resisted the urge to roll my eyes. Of course, he was thinking of anything apart from the well-being of his children.

"Everything will be resolved by the end of the day," Lady Audley said. "You go make your preparations. Alice will have a quick chat with the police, and then we'll figure everything out with Peterson."

Saracen opened his mouth as if to protest, but then snapped it shut and looked at me, confusion in his eyes.

The female police officer emerged from the castle, her expression tight. "Lady Audley, has Princess Alice moved bedrooms?"

"No, she's always used the same room."

"She's not in there. Any idea where she might be?"

"Did you try the bathroom? It's the room next door to her bedroom," Lady Audley said.

"We looked in most of the rooms on that floor, and she's not in any of them."

I breathed a quiet sigh of relief. Campbell had done it. He'd gotten Alice out of the castle without anyone seeing.

"She won't be far," Lady Audley said. "I'll go and find her."

Ten minutes of increasingly anxious searching, and Alice was still nowhere to be found.

The police were looking worried, and even Lady Audley seemed pensive.

"She's not answering her phone," Rupert said. "And I've sent her several text messages. Where could she be?"

I remained silent and tried to look as worried as everyone else. It wasn't hard. Alice was very much not in the clear, and I was still undecided if her running was the wisest move.

"We need to do a top-to-bottom search of the castle," the female officer said. "With your permission, Lord and Lady Audley."

"Well, this isn't our home, but I'm sure it won't be a problem. There are no secrets inside. I'm sure Alice is playing the fool. Perhaps she thinks this is a game, and she's hiding."

"This is no game," the female officer said. "Evading the police won't do her any favors."

"She's not evading the police," Peterson said. "The child is just confused."

I hated the way they spoke about Alice as if she was a twelve-year-old girl with no clue about how the world worked. She had moments when her head was in the clouds, but she was smart, funny, and deserved to be talked about much better than this.

"We could do with some assistance to cover this place quickly," the female police officer said to Saracen.

"I'll get some of the team on it." Saracen glanced at me, questions hovering in his eyes, but I'd reveal nothing until it was safe to do so.

The search took almost forty-five minutes, and by the end of it, everyone was convinced Alice was no longer inside the castle.

Peterson was speaking quietly to Lord and Lady Audley, and I stepped closer to hear what he had to say.

"This doesn't look good. She should have stayed where she was."

"I was going to speak to her this morning," Lady Audley said. "I didn't think she'd do anything this stupid."

"Can't we say it's her poor health making her behave this way?" Lord Audley said. "She ran because she doesn't understand what was going on."

"I'll try to spin this in our favor," Peterson said. "And I'd like to have a look at her annual health assessment. There could be something in there to support our case."

I couldn't hold my tongue any longer as I marched closer. "Alice isn't crazy. And she'd hate you for doing this."

Peterson turned, his brow furrowed. "We appreciate your concern, but this is the easiest way to help Princess Alice. I've done this before, and it always works. And if we don't do this, Princess Alice is at risk of going to prison."

"She won't go to prison, because she didn't kill anyone," I said. "If you believed in her, you'd do your job properly and defend her, not look for a loophole and assume the worst."

"That's enough," Lady Audley said. "She's our daughter and we're looking out for her."

"Are you, really? You don't seem to know any-thing about Alice. It would break her heart that you're treating her like this."

"It would break my heart if my daughter went to prison," Lady Audley said. "Alice needs pro-tecting from herself sometimes. How long have you known her?"

"Long enough," I said.

Lady Audley shook her head. "Alice is prone to fits of fancy that don't befit her status. Why do you think we've had so much trouble making a suitable match for her? The men who get to know her see there's something not quite right."

"Not quite right? Alice is amazing." Her parents really had no clue about her. "Perhaps Alice is already in love, but she's scared you'll judge her match, the way you're judging me and Rupert."

Lady Audley's face paled. "We haven't judged you. We're giving you a fair chance."

"I don't know about fair, but you seem to enjoy pointing out my failings. I'll admit, I'm not perfect, and I've always considered myself not good enough for Rupert, but he insists he loves me, and I care very much for him. I want to make him happy, but I'm not sure I can do that if you don't approve of me. And as for Alice not being able to find a suitable match, it's got nothing to do with her health." I bit my tongue before I blurted out Campbell's name.

"I've had enough of this nonsense," Lady Audley said. "Let's take this conversation inside. We won't be bothered anymore by outsiders." The three of them turned and walked away.

Anger simmered through me. This was all about reputation and maintaining the status quo for them. It had nothing to do with what was best for Alice. They were treating her like she was a broken commodity they had to patch up before their reputations were damaged.

Someone cleared their throat behind me, and I turned to see Saracen.

"That was quite a performance, Holly," he said.

"It wasn't a performance. I can't believe they're doing this to Alice."

"Don't hold it against them," Saracen said. "Take a walk with me. You need to burn off that anger before you do something you'll really regret."

"I don't have time for a walk. I have to stop Alice's parents from making her out to be insane and find the real killer."

"Five minutes won't hurt. You need to focus, and you're too angry to think straight. Let's move." He grabbed my arm and marched me away from the castle.

I took a few deep breaths, still furious about the way I'd been spoken to by Rupert's parents.

"Did you know, Campbell studied under a Tibetan yogi for two years?" Saracen said.

I was so surprised I almost stumbled over my own feet. "Any time I've mentioned meditation to help with his stress levels, he's grunted at me. You're telling me he's an experienced practitioner?"

"Yep. He does it every day. He makes all of us do it too. He says you need a quiet, focused mind to work effectively. If the background noise gets in the way of your mission, you'll make a mistake and someone could get hurt."

"He really is a man of mystery. But why are you telling me this about Campbell?"

"Because you need to follow that advice. This situation is hard for you. Your best friend and your gran are suspects in this investigation. Plus, you could potentially become an Audley, and you're locking horns with the people you're supposed to be making nice with."

"I know all that, but I have no choice. I'm protecting Alice."

Saracen was quiet as we continued to walk. "You're a great friend to her, so I'm only going to ask you this once. Do you know anything about her disappearance?"

I squeezed my eyes shut for a second. I didn't want to lie to Saracen.

"Silence is often more incriminating than someone babbling a made-up story to cover their tracks. You helped to get her out of the castle, didn't you?"

I looked over my shoulder to make sure no one could hear us. "In a roundabout way."

Saracen groaned. "It was Campbell. I knew something was up when he was talking to you. He's taken Alice somewhere so she won't be arrested."

"Yes, he has. But we have to keep this to ourselves."

"This won't help Alice."

"That's what I argued initially, but he wouldn't listen. And after seeing how Alice's parents were talking about her, I'm now thinking it was the right thing to do."

"The police won't agree." He pulled out his phone and called a number. "Campbell's phone has been disconnected. Why am I not surprised? He knows how to hide."

"Campbell's in love, and he's protecting his girl. We need to give him a chance to help her. With Alice out of the way, we can figure out how to save her, not just muddle through with what the lawyer has in mind and send her to an insane asylum."

"I hate that idea, too. Alice doesn't deserve that."

"Alice will hate it. She's always trying to impress her parents. Whether it's learning to sing, play an instrument, or paint. The whole time I've worked here, she's been looking at ways to get them to notice her. Now, all they want to do is label her crazy and send her away. It's her worst fear come true."

"So what do you want to do? How are we going to show Alice is innocent?"

"Reggie Frasier is the prime suspect in my mind. We have to go after him and get him talking."

"He's staying in the castle. He's in the guest wing with some of the other wedding guests."

"Then that's where we need to be." I turned to hurry back to the castle, but Saracen caught hold of my arm.

"Are you feeling more focused?"

"I'm less angry. I don't want to say anything rude to my future in-laws, if that's what you're asking."

"It's good enough. Let's move."

We turned and raced back to the castle.

Saracen's phone rang, and he pulled it out, sighing as he checked the caller display. "I thought it was Campbell. It's the Duchess. I need to give her an update on what's going on."

"Are you going to tell her Campbell ran off with Alice?"

He grimaced. "I should."

"The fewer people who know, the better. The Duchess is on Alice's side, but I'm not sure how she'll feel about keeping this news to herself. And I don't want her getting on the bad side of Lord and Lady Audley. What she doesn't know won't hurt her."

"Agreed. I won't say anything for now." Saracen answered the call.

Time was definitely not on our side. If I didn't solve this murder soon, it would be too late for Alice and Campbell.

"Understood," Saracen said. "I'm on my way back. I'll come straight to you." He ended the call and looked at me. "The Duchess wants to see me now, but I should come with you to talk to Reggie."

"Go look after the Duchess. I can handle Reggie."

"Handle him carefully. Remember what I said about him being a criminal?"

"I haven't forgotten. I'll come find you as soon as I've got anything useful on him."

"Same here. And let me know the second you hear anything from either Alice or Campbell."

"Will do." I raced around the side of the castle with Meatball. I wanted to sneak in through a side door to make sure Lord and Lady Audley didn't see me. The last thing I needed was another confrontation.

I dashed around a tall hedge and slammed straight into Chef Heston.

Chapter 12

"Holly! Where have you been hiding? You're over an hour late for work," Chef Heston said.

I tried to dodge around him, but he stepped into my path. "I'm sorry. There's a family emergency. I need to go. I'll make it up to you."

"Stop right there. I deserve an explanation. We have ten coachloads of tourists arriving at the castle today, and I can't be without your cakes."

"You'll have to use what's in the fridge. And there's frozen tea loaf you can defrost. If you do it now, it should be ready for the lunchtime rush."

He held up his hand. "Frozen tea loaf is not good enough. If you still want your job, you're going to that kitchen right now."

"I do want my job. But ..." I had to get inside the castle and speak to Reggie.

Chef Heston huffed out a breath. "I understand you're in a relationship with Lord Rupert, and I'm happy for you, but you need to let me know if you're not going to keep working for me. You can't start coming and going as you please because you're about to become a member of the family. You owe me that much. I've taught you a lot since you've been here, and I deserve some respect."

I sucked in a breath, all my emotions bubbling to the surface. "I respect you, Chef Heston. I love working here. Even though you can be grumpy and tell me off for not paying enough attention—"

"You're digging your own grave by insulting me," he said. "I will fire you. If you push me too far, you're out."

A sob slipped from my lips. "It's all a mess. Alice, her horrible parents, my gran's wedding, and her friend being murdered."

"I heard about that. I'm sorry your gran lost a friend, but—"

"It's not just that. They think Alice is guilty of murder. The police want to take her away. Now she's vanished, and, and ..."

"Take a breath. You say Princess Alice has vanished? Where's she gone? And no one will believe she killed that woman. She may be ditzy, but she's the sweetest young woman I've ever met."

"I barely have time to breathe. Gran and Ray's wedding was ruined. Daphne was killed, Alice looks guilty, but she's not. Now, Lord and Lady Audley are here and they're horrible. And I don't want horrible in-laws. I want a mother-in-law I can have fun with. Someone who'll be an amazing grandmother to my children. I'm not sure about any of it. And what about Rupert? I don't want to hurt him, but I can't sit by and let his family steamroller Alice into a spa with straitjackets."

"You lost me a dozen sentences ago. What's this about Rupert and straitjackets?"

I swallowed another sob. "Rupert says he loves me, but does he? How can you love someone who's such a bad fit for your family? And I was looking forward to Alice being my bridesmaid. And now none of that will happen. If her parents get their way, they'll lock her up and I'll never see her again. I have to stop that. And what about Campbell? I can't do this on my own."

Chef Heston stepped forward and wrapped me in a tight hug.

I gasped, so surprised by his action that I lost the power of speech. Which was a good thing, given the nonsense coming out of my mouth.

It was only then that I realized I was shaking, had a terrible headache, and felt dizzy.

"Breathe deeply, in and out, and relax. You're heading into full-on panic attack mode if you're not careful." Chef Heston kept hold of me as he spoke. It was a warm, safe feeling, fatherly hug.

My teeth chattered together, and I closed my eyes. My head was a mess, and I didn't know how to handle the chaos around me.

Chef Heston patted me on the back. "Holly, you're an amazing baker. I don't want to lose you from my kitchen. If anything, I'm jealous because the family is taking you away from me." He stepped back, keeping hold of my shoulders.

"You're jealous?"

"Don't be so surprised. You make incredible cakes. You're talented, bright, and quick to learn. And yes, sometimes I can be surly with you, but that's because I know how good you are, and you're only getting better. I push you because I know you can handle it. You work so well under pressure."

"Not this time," I said. "I've messed everything up. I've failed you, my future in-laws don't like me, and Alice and my gran are in trouble."

"And you can fix all of that. I know it's not just baking you thrive on. You're an amazing sleuth. Don't think I haven't noticed you snooping around when there's trouble at the castle and sneaking off to investigate things you should have nothing to do with."

"I didn't think you noticed. I thought I was being discreet. It never affected my work."

"I know it didn't. But I notice everything that happens in my kitchen. And do you know why I didn't yell at you about it too often?"

"I'm hoping it's because you like me."

A rare smile crossed his face. "Because I knew you were doing it for the right reasons. You're always getting involved because you want to help people. You love this castle and you love this family, and you want to protect them. That makes you a good person. I will not stand in the way of someone who's trying to do the right thing."

"Oh! I don't know what to say." Tears filled my eyes, and I blinked them away.

"I want you to say you'll keep working for me. I want you to keep producing those incredible cakes."

"I'll do that. I don't want to leave the kitchen, no matter what happens, or who I marry."

"If you marry Lord Rupert, the arrangements will have to change. A member of the Audley family won't fit in as a kitchen assistant."

"Does that mean you're giving me a promotion?"

He snorted a laugh. "No, but I've been thinking. Perhaps you can set up your own company making cakes. How about calling it Audley

Artistry Eats? No, that's a terrible name. We can work on that."

I hadn't expected that response. "You think I could really do that?"

"You ran your own business before, why not again? You're clever enough and determined enough to make anything happen when you put your mind to it."

"I always knew you secretly liked me."

He grunted out a laugh. "You're so much more than you realize, not just in the kitchen, but in life. Now, what are you standing around here for? Don't you have Alice and your gran to protect?"

"I do, but I'm scared you're going to fire me."

"Your job is safe. Go and save them. That's an order."

I kissed him on the cheek. "Thanks, Chef Heston. You're the best."

He grumbled under his breath as I raced off with Meatball. Having emotionally exploded all over Chef Heston, I felt much more grounded. I had a long list of problems to tackle, but if I focused on one at a time, I could solve them all.

And my first problem was Reggie.

I dashed up the back stairs of the castle. It was a stone staircase, mainly used by the servants to get around when they were cleaning, and headed into the guest wing.

I knocked at a few doors, and at my fourth door, I discovered Reggie's room.

He stared at me, his eyes cold. "I've already had my room turned down, and I don't need any room service."

"Good, because I'm not here to clean your room, or feed you. I need to talk to you about Daphne."

His gaze traveled over me. "Oh, it's you. You were at the wedding."

"That's right. Daphne was my gran's friend. I'm Holly."

"What do you want?" He stood in the doorway, his arms crossed.

There was no time for niceties. "I want to know if you murdered Daphne."

Reggie stared hard at me. I stared right back. I couldn't afford to waste a second being friendly, or winkle the information out of him with delicious cakes and kind words. I had to know the truth.

Reggie glanced out the door, looking either way along the corridor. He grabbed my shoulder and yanked me inside, slamming the door shut and leaving Meatball in the corridor.

Meatball barked and pawed at the door, not happy at being left behind.

"Why are you pointing the finger at me?" Reggie asked. "I heard some princess is in the frame for Daphne's murder."

"Tell me about your relationship with Daphne."

"Why?"

"Because Princess Alice is innocent. And I need the police to stop asking my gran questions."

He grunted. "They reckon it was one of them who killed Daphne, though?"

"They're both on the suspect list, and I'm not happy about that. Tell me about Daphne."

Reggie shrugged. "There's nothing to tell. We were fine. Rolling along until something better happened."

"Don't lie to me. I heard you on the phone. You've got another woman on the go. And you said you wanted to get rid of Daphne."

"That was the drink talking. We were happy. We even talked about marriage a few times."

"I don't believe that either. Daphne was miserable with you. She wanted to get away. Was that why you hurt her?"

"She told you that?"

"She told Gran, and I trust her. Did you kill Daphne?"

Reggie's mouth twisted into a snarl. "Be careful what you say. I don't like being accused of something I didn't do."

"I'm not scared of you. I know about your past."

"If you know so much, why are you being so dumb and coming after me? I can make people disappear."

"So can I. There are acres of grounds out there that people rarely walk around. It would be easy to hide a body out there. And I work in the kitchen, so I have access to lots of sharp knives and a meat grinder."

He spluttered out a laugh. "You're threatening to turn me into hamburger meat?"

"My gran's friend is dead, my best friend is in the frame for murder, and my gran's also been questioned by the police, so yes, if I have to threaten you to get the truth, then that's what I'll do."

"I could kill you right now, and no-one would know what happened to you. You'd just be another insignificant missing person."

"They would. People know I'm here. And my dog is right outside this door, barking. If you make me disappear, my gran will hunt you down."

Reggie stared at me for another second, then tipped back his head and roared out a laugh. "You are something else. I see how you're related to Molly. I haven't had such fun in ages. A little thing like you threatening to dump my body in the woods, or turn me into mince-meat. That's classic."

"I'm glad you find me amusing. But you need to tell me everything that happened the night Daphne died."

He took off his jacket and placed it on the bed. "I'll talk. You've got me so scared, I'll say anything."

"I'm not joking."

Reggie glanced at me and some of the humor on his face faded. "Sure, I get it. Family is important. You're looking out for your gran, and I respect that."

"So, Daphne. Were there problems between you?"

Reggie settled in a seat by the bed. "A few. We were thinking about calling time on our relationship."

"Was that a joint decision? Did Daphne know about the woman you were seeing?"

"She may have done, I didn't exactly keep it a secret. Just like Daphne didn't keep it a secret she was fooling around on me. She'd been doing it for ages."

"Who was Daphne fooling around with?"

"Any guy she liked the look of. I didn't mind if she was discreet, but Daphne got careless. It wouldn't surprise me if she met up with someone and he roughed her up."

"I'm still interested in you, not a mystery man who may not even exist. You're open about your past, and you must have a temper if you don't mind hurting people to get them to see your way."

"I only hurt those who deserve it, and I'd never hit a woman. That's a scumbag move, and I ain't no scumbag. The morals of the mob may not be wholesome, but we look after our women. If I'd messed up Daphne, the guys would have seen to it that I didn't have functioning kneecaps. I know where to draw the line. We argued a lot and our relationship was fiery. I'd had enough and wanted out. So did Daphne. We only hung out together because it was convenient."

"Daphne didn't have anything on you? You didn't need to keep her quiet because she knew something about your shady connections?"

He grinned. "Shady connections? Daphne was as shady as they came. Did you know, your gran met Daphne when she was in prison?"

"I know that. How did you meet her?"

"At a bar. She was a real looker in her day. We had fun together, but were both ready to move on. And since I'm being all open and honest with you, whoever bumped her off did me a favor. It meant there was no messy split, and it's all done with."

"Where were you when Daphne was killed?"

"The police have already talked to me about this, and I've given them my alibi. I was outside having a cigar."

"On your own?"

"There were other people around, but we weren't paying each other much attention. If you like, you can go and check to see where I stubbed out my cigar. I used a big stone urn out the back. I told the cops to take a look and swab for my DNA. I'm on their system, but I doubt they'll bother. Why would they, since they've got that princess?"

"They don't have her," I said. "And Alice is innocent."

"Whatever you say. I'm done with this place, and I want out of here. As soon as the police give me the green light, you won't see me for dust."

I took a breath. "Since it wasn't Alice, or my gran, or you if you're to be believed—"

"Which I am."

"Who do you think killed Daphne?"

"If it wasn't a guy she hooked up with at the wedding, you should speak to that harpy of a daughter. She hated Daphne."

"I didn't know Daphne had any children. Was she invited to the wedding?"

"Her name's Kate, and she didn't get an official invite, but Daphne called her to come to the castle."

"Why would she do that?"

"It beats me. I always found it better not to question Daphne. All I know is she was talking to Kate on the phone, and then said she'd be coming to the castle."

"What was their relationship like?"

"Bad. Kate hated everything about her mother. She hated her criminal past and the fact she was dating me. Daphne couldn't do any-thing right by her."

"Is Kate still around?" Saracen hadn't men-tioned a daughter being in the picture.

"She'll be about. If I were you, I'd take a close look at her. She always had a nasty look in her eye. I'd catch her looking at Daphne and you could tell she was thinking dark thoughts. She's not a nice woman."

"I'll speak to her. You're not going anywhere, are you? I may have more questions."

"Until the police say so, I'm staying put and not causing trouble. And if the family keeps giving me free room and board, I have no complaints. But I'm not staying any longer than I have to."

I was still suspicious of Reggie, but I had no way of confirming his alibi since the police were no longer talking to me via Campbell. But Reggie had given me another avenue to investigate, and I needed all the suspects I could gather to clear Alice's name and make sure the police didn't circle back to Gran.

After a quick goodbye, I left the room and collected Meatball from outside the door.

"Let's go, boy. We have another suspect to speak to."

Chapter 13

I almost collided with Saracen as I walked out of the castle. If he hadn't caught the door with a firm hand, it would have slammed into his face.

"I've got news about Reggie. And I also found out Daphne has a daughter," I said.

Saracen swiped a hand across his forehead. "Great. I ... uh, that's good."

My gaze ran over him. "Are you feeling okay?"

"I'm fine. I just haven't had a chance to rest since I took over this investigation. The family is pressing hard for a quick resolution." Saracen was pale, sweaty, and his hands were shaking.

"Don't lie. You're not looking after yourself. When did you last eat? And what was it?"

"I can't worry about eating right at the moment. Campbell needs me."

"And you need to look after your blood sugar levels. Come with me. We're getting something to eat and drink and then sitting down to discuss our next move."

"Holly! We don't have time. Isn't that what you keep telling me?"

"We do! I'm not letting you get sick. I can't do this all on my own. Follow me." I strode off toward the café with Meatball. A few seconds later, Saracen caught up with us.

"I don't want to look like I'm slacking on the job," he said. "And Lord and Lady Audley are moving fast, so neither Alice nor Campbell have much time."

"You need to get your blood sugar stable. You'll be no good to anyone if you fall into a diabetic coma." We entered the café, and I pointed at a table in the corner where it wasn't too busy. "Sit down. I'll be right back." I dashed into the kitchen.

"Are you here to work?" Chef Heston said the second he spotted me. "Is everything okay with Princess Alice?"

"Oh, no! But I will make it up to you, I promise."

"Then get what you need and get out of my way," he said.

I grabbed a box of the low sugar flapjacks I'd been perfecting and hurried back into the café. I made two strong coffees from the self-serve machine and returned to the table where Saracen sat.

"You eat, I'll talk," I said as I settled opposite him. I pulled off the lid of the container and offered the flapjacks to him.

He grabbed two and took a large bite of one, chewing furiously.

I sipped my coffee and let my thoughts settle. "I saw Reggie. At first, he wasn't friendly, but after I threatened him—"

"You threatened Reggie Frasier?"

"Eat, don't talk. I did. I figured that was his language. He found it funny. Then he started opening up."

"What did he tell you about Daphne?"

"He said they were having problems and thinking about splitting up."

"He told the police the same thing. What else?"

"Reggie said he was outside smoking when Daphne was killed, although he's not sure anyone saw him. Have you learned any more about her time of death and how she died?"

"She was hit twice over the head. The blow to the front of her temple killed her. And the marks are a match for the bottle of wine found in Princess Alice's hand. Daphne couldn't have been dead more than half an hour when she was discovered."

"What about any fingerprints on the bottle?" I asked.

Saracen shook his head. "Not helpful. Only Alice's."

"No one else's? Isn't that odd? Surely, the bottle must have been handled by other people."

"It was the vintage being served at your gran's wedding reception," Saracen said. "It must have been taken off one of the tables. Whoever used it on Daphne wiped it clean before leaving it with Alice."

"Have any wedding guests confirmed seeing Reggie outside at the time of the murder?" I said. "I still think he's good for this."

"Not so far, and the police are more interested in finding evidence to show Princess Alice's guilt, especially now she's run off."

"Then she needs to keep running. If they're focused on her, they won't look at anyone else."

"At least it's good news for your gran. If they're targeting Princess Alice, they won't come after her."

I nodded. "It's one problem solved. Campbell will keep them hidden for as long as they need to." I studied Saracen's complexion. He was less gray and sweaty. "How are you feeling?"

"Your food is already working its magic," he said. "Thanks for looking out for me."

"Keep the flapjacks on you. If you're not taking proper breaks, then you need to stay fueled for this task."

"I didn't even notice I wasn't feeling so good. I'm worried the police know Campbell was involved in taking Alice."

"What have they said to you?"

"Nothing directly, but they've asked me a couple of times where Campbell is. I just keep saying he no longer works for the family, but they're not buying it. They're closing ranks because they think the whole team has been compromised."

"Campbell needs to be careful, or he could lose his job over this."

"Or worse. The police won't think kindly of him if he's helping someone they consider a criminal."

"The crazy things people do for love."

Saracen snorted a laugh. "You'd be just the same if Lord Rupert was up on a murder charge."

I shrugged. "Most likely. Okay, let's focus on a new suspect. Do you know anything about Daphne's daughter, Kate?"

"Yes, I've been in touch with her. She's on her way back to the castle as we speak. Daphne had some personal effects that need collecting, so Kate's coming to get them."

"How did she take the news of her mother's murder?"

"She's been remarkably calm about it. She asked a few questions but didn't sound upset when I spoke to her on the phone. She said they weren't close, even though they lived together."

"Reggie said Kate hated her mother, and they often argued."

"Do you think the daughter had something to do with Daphne's death?" Saracen said. "If they weren't close, I can understand her not being upset that she's gone."

"She could be involved. Maybe she wanted her mother dead so she could get her hands on her assets. It sounds like she's quick enough to come here to get Daphne's things."

Saracen's phone buzzed, and he checked the message. "We'll know soon enough, because she's almost here."

"I want to speak to her," I said.

He grinned. "I figured you would. That's why I was coming to find you."

"Are you sure you're up to this?" Saracen's hands were still shaking. "I can always talk to Kate on my own if you're not feeling good."

"Not a chance. Even if Kate had nothing to do with Daphne's murder, she could give us insight on Reggie, or someone else from Daphne's past who wanted her dead."

"Reggie's opinion of Kate was bad. And he also told me Kate came here the night of the wedding."

"She lives thirty miles from here, so it would have been easy to do. Why was she here?"

"That's something we need to find out."

Could we be onto something with Kate? An angry daughter who stumbled on a chance to get rid of her mother? This suspect had just gotten more interesting.

We finished our coffees, and I made sure Saracen ate another flapjack before putting the rest in his pockets. Then we headed out of the café and to the main parking lot where Kate was arriving.

"I said I'd meet her at the main entrance gates," Saracen said. "Kate said she won't be able to stay for long because she can't take much time off work."

"She really doesn't sound cut up about her mother being dead."

"Some people aren't close to their parents," Saracen said. "That's all it could be."

"Or it could be we've found ourselves a new prime suspect. Although I'm not letting Reggie off the hook just yet."

Five minutes later, a compact black car pulled to a halt beside us. The window slid down. A woman in her mid-thirties with her hair scraped off her face in a ponytail peered out. "Are you Saracen?"

"That's right. You must be Kate Chamberlain."

"I use my father's surname. I'm Kate Reynolds. Where shall I park?"

"Any of the spaces are fine."

We waited for Kate to parallel park before she climbed out of the car. She wore a plain blue pantsuit with a white shirt underneath. She hurried over to us. "Where are my mother's things?"

"Nothing's been touched in her room," Saracen said. "I thought you might like to look through them and decide what you want to keep."

She sighed. "Most of it can probably be thrown in the trash. I hope to be able to do this quickly. I've only got the afternoon off work."

"Of course. I'll show you to her room," Saracen said.

"Very well. Let's get this over with." She glanced at me. "Are you some sort of helper?"

"I'm Holly. I knew Daphne. She was friends with my gran."

Kate shrugged. "And ..."

"I wanted to ask you a few questions about Daphne if you've got the time."

"So long as you can walk and talk." She looked at Saracen. "Show me the way."

I hurried along beside Kate. "I'm sorry about what happened to your mother."

"Oh, don't be. Something like this was bound to happen to her, eventually."

"I'm not sure what you mean."

Kate slid me a glance. "How much do you know about her past?"

"I know a little. I know she was in prison for a while."

"Then you can understand why it's no surprise she came to a sticky end. My mother attracted trouble. She enjoyed making life difficult for people, me included. You go around doing that too much, and eventually, you find someone who causes you even more trouble. I expect she started a fight with someone and they got her back."

"Were you close?"

Kate shrugged. "Not really."

"But you lived together?"

"We did. It was mainly for convenience, and my mother was rarely there, so it was almost like having my own place. She used to come and go as she liked. Our relationship felt the wrong way round. I was the mother, and she was the inconsiderate daughter who'd stumble home drunk in the early hours of the morning with some random man on her arm."

"Was she dating anyone special?"

"None of the men my mother dated were special. And you know what I said about trouble. The guys she fooled around with were the very definition of that word." Kate leaned closer. "Her most regular guy, Reggie, used to work for the mob. She thought it was exciting. But all it was, was sad and ridiculous. Especially given her advancing years."

We entered the castle and headed up to the guest wing.

"Even though your mother sounds like she had a fire in her, I imagine you still helped her when she needed you," I said.

Kate shook her head. "For my sins, I helped when I had to. She was family. It was my obligation."

"Was that why you came to the castle during the wedding reception?"

"You seem to know an awful lot about my movements," Kate said.

"I want to make sure my gran's friend gets justice. I'm sure you feel the same. You must want to know what happened to your mother."

"It's this room." Saracen stopped outside a door.

Kate pushed the door open and stepped into the room. She glanced around. "Was this where it happened?"

The blood stain on the carpet was already gone and the room was set to right. It looked like nothing bad had ever happened in here.

"That's right," Saracen said. "If you need some time alone, I understand. This must be hard for you."

"No, it's not a problem. If you've got a bag I can use to put her things in, that would be helpful."

"Your mother's case is over by the bed," Saracen said. "I don't think she had anything else with her."

"What about the jewelry she wore?" Kate heaved the case onto the bed. She flipped it open, rifled around for a few seconds, then headed to the drawers and opened them. She pulled out a few things and tossed them into the case.

"The personal items on her body will be sent to you as soon as possible." Saracen glanced at me and raised his eyebrows.

"Good. So long as I get them. She owes me. She was always begging money off me. I've kept a tally, so I know what I'm entitled to."

Kate really was charmless when talking about her deceased mother. "Why were you here the night of the wedding?"

"Because my mother was being irresponsible again. She'd forgotten to bring her blood pressure medication. I was forced to abandon a date and drive here so I could give it to her. I shouldn't have wasted my time, given what happened."

"We have to look out for our family," I said. "Even when they misbehave."

"She rarely looked out for me. She was too busy having fun and messing around with any guy who took her eye. And it was like there was a competition between Reggie and my mother to see who could cheat the most. It was pathetic." Kate slapped the case lid shut. "It was most likely a jealous girlfriend who killed her, or one of her many lovers. She had so many, I lost count."

"Was there anyone your mother was seeing regularly other than Reggie?" I said. "Maybe someone who got possessive and wanted her to himself."

"Not that I know of, but I tended not to listen when she told me about her lurid adventures with random men." Kate paused from rifling through the bedside cabinet and looked at me. "You know, she even told me she'd had fun with a guy in the band playing at the wedding. It's the sort of thing a teenager would do. She was bragging about it on the phone like it was something special, and I was supposed to be impressed."

"Did she tell you the name of this guy?"

"If she did, I don't remember. I had no interest in that side of her life." Kate slammed the bedside cabinet shut. "I don't think there's anything else here." She glanced at me. "You probably think I'm cold, not crying and saying I miss my mother, but I've been her unpaid servant most of my life. I'm thirty-five and deserve my freedom. I've had enough of chasing around after her and making sure she looked after herself. My mother wasn't an easy person to be around, she had a strong personality. You know what I felt when I got the call from the police to say she was dead?"

"Sad?"

"Relieved. I'm long overdue being free from her nonsense. I deserve better. Now, I get the chance to live my life, my way. I won't ever have to wait for the late-night phone call from my mother as she drunkenly giggles and tells me what she's been up to. You can think what you like about me. But she was a terrible mother."

"I'm sorry your relationship was bad," I said. "I hope you find peace now she's gone."

"I will. Last night was the first decent night's sleep I've had in a long time, and all because I didn't have her to worry about." Kate nodded at Saracen. "You know where I am if you need to speak to me again." She picked up the case and walked out the door.

Saracen tilted his head, his eyes wide. "That was interesting. I'd say Daphne and her daughter were the dominant personality type."

"I understand why she's being so blunt. If Daphne was such a terrible mother, Kate won't shed tears over her. Have you been able to check her alibi?"

"I've got the team looking through the CCTV for the time Kate was here. If that checks out, we can rule her off the suspect list."

I nodded. "She does have a motive. If her mother was treating her badly, she may have pushed her too far. Kate turned up angry, and they fought."

"I'll let you know when I hear anything from the team."

"Even if it wasn't Kate, I'm glad we talked to her," I said. "She's given me someone else as a suspect."

"Who's that?"

"The night of Gran and Ray's wedding, I saw the lead guitarist in Pearl's band come out of the closet. He wasn't alone, not if his rumpled shirt or the lipstick smeared across his cheek was anything to go by."

"You think he was fooling around with Daphne?"

I nodded. "I need to ask him that, but first I have to check on my gran and Ray, see how they're doing after the horrible end to their wedding."

"You do that. I'll check in with my team about Kate's alibi. Do you know the name of the guy in the band?"

"Jed. Only a first name. I'd recognize him, though, and Pearl will have his details. I'll pass them on when I can, then you can run a background check."

Saracen grinned at me. "Great minds think alike. Speak to you soon, partner."

Chapter 14

I slowed as I approached my apartment with Meatball. Ray was walking along the path, his shoulders down and a bag in his hand.

Meatball gave a happy bark when he spotted him and dashed ahead of me.

"Ray, is everything okay?" I asked as I caught up with Meatball.

He shook his head, despair written across his face. "I don't know what's going on. Your gran's just chucked me out."

I laughed. "Sure she has. You're teasing me."

He shook his head. "This is no joke. She's been acting strangely. I kept asking her what was wrong, but she wouldn't talk to me. Then she said I needed to leave. She needed a break from me."

"Did you leave the toilet seat up again?"

"I don't think I did anything wrong. The wedding was great, other than what happened to Daphne, and we've been talking about the honeymoon. We spoke to the holiday company, and they agreed we can push the dates back. The police don't want your gran leaving the country until the murder is solved. Although we didn't mention that when we adjusted our plans."

"Is that what's making Gran unhappy? You've had to postpone your honeymoon."

"She was fine about it. We both grumbled a bit, but we understand why it had to happen. And she doesn't want to go anywhere until the murder is solved."

"The police are much more interested in Alice than Gran for this murder, so hopefully they won't mind when you do get away."

"Maybe there won't be a honeymoon. Not if she doesn't want me around."

"Did Gran say anything about what's worrying her?"

"She was talking about Daphne and the fact she always buys the same outfits as her. It used to get her so mad. Then she went quiet and disappeared into the bedroom for a while. I thought she'd gone for a lie down, but then she came out with this bag and said I had to leave."

"This must be a mistake. Ray, come back with me and we'll talk to her together. She's got the wrong end of the stick about something. Gran must be under a lot of stress, given what happened to Daphne."

"No, I want to give her some space, that's what she wants. I wish she'd just tell me what's going on, though. I'm her husband. I'm supposed to be there to help."

I gave him a hug. "I'll go talk to her, see what's happening. Don't worry, you'll have your feet back under the table in no time." I kissed his cheek, then hurried to the apartment.

I turned and watched Ray walk away. What was going on with Gran? She'd never shoved Ray away before.

I tried the handle, but the door was locked from the inside. I pulled out my key and tried it. It turned, but I still couldn't get the door to open.

"Gran, it's Holly. What are you up to? I can't get in the front door. If you're worried about Ray, he's gone." Maybe this dispute was more serious than I'd thought if Gran had blocked the door.

A few seconds later, there was a scraping sound from the other side of the door.

Gran inched it open and peeked out. "Are you alone?"

"Other than Meatball. I just saw Ray. Why have you kicked him out?"

Gran pulled the door open wider, giving me enough room to get inside. She grabbed hold of my arm and yanked me in, shutting the door the second Meatball was through the gap.

It was gloomy in the apartment. The curtains were drawn and no lights on.

"Why are you sneaking about in the dark?" I went to open the curtains, but she grabbed my hand.

"Don't do that."

"Gran, you're being weird. Talk to me. What's happening? Why have you kicked Ray out?"

She pressed a finger to her lips, then gestured me into the living room. I walked in to find a selection of knives on the table.

"I take it you're not planning a cookery demonstration," I said. "Why have you got my best knives on display?"

Gran hurried to the window. She peeked around the side of the curtain, then returned to me. "It's not safe. You shouldn't be here."

"I live here. And why isn't it safe?"

Gran paced the room, Saffron trotting at her heel, whining softly as if she could sense my gran's distress.

I collected up the knives. "They can't stay here. The dogs might hurt themselves."

"We need to place them around the apartment so we have weapons easily to hand."

"Why do we need weapons?"

She sighed. "Because I think whoever killed Daphne was really after me."

I was so shocked I almost dropped the knives. I hurried into the kitchen, set them down on the counter out of the reach of the dogs, then returned to Gran. "Talk to me. Why do you think that? Has someone threatened you?"

"No, but I've been thinking about what happened at the reception. We look the same from behind, everyone says so. And at the wedding, we had the same evening outfit on. Do you remember, we argued about it?"

"Of course I do. But no one wants you dead."

"I'm not so sure about that. I have enemies in my past."

"No, Gran, you're worrying about nothing. It was Reggie or Daphne's daughter Kate who killed her. Saracen is checking Kate's alibi as we speak."

"Kate? I didn't think they talked to each other. Daphne couldn't stand the girl. She said Kate always thought she was better than her."

"Take a seat, let me explain what's going on. And you need to stop panicking and placing weapons around the place. No one is out to get you."

Gran perched on the couch, and I sat next to her. "Why do you think it was Kate?"

"She was here the night Daphne was killed, and she didn't hide the fact she hated her mother. Daphne called her and asked her to bring her blood pressure medication to the wedding reception because she'd forgotten it."

Gran waved a hand in the air. "Daphne was always doing that. I lost count of the number of times she forgot her medication when we went out. I didn't know she'd contacted Kate, though."

"They lived together."

"They did? I thought Daphne lived with Reggie."

"Not according to Kate. And she wasn't happy about being dragged away from a date to help her mother. She told me some unpleasant things about Daphne, including that she was glad her mother was dead. She felt free."

Gran was quiet for a moment. "I know they had a bad relationship. Kate came to visit Daphne a few times when she was in prison. She was awful to her. The visits stopped after Kate started a yelling match in the visitors' room. She was banned from seeing her mother after that."

"What did she yell at her about?"

"Mainly that Daphne was an embarrassment. It got ugly. Both of them were yelling and screaming and throwing around accusations. Kate even slapped her mother in the face. Prison guards came over and marched Kate away. And that was it. She wasn't allowed to visit Daphne anymore."

"Daphne must have been upset about what happened between them."

"If she was, she never confided in me about it. Their relationship was weird, and there was no fondness between them. Daphne even said she regretted ever having children. She didn't like Kate one bit. She called her a shrew and said Kate had no idea how to have fun."

"So you won't be surprised to learn Kate wasn't shedding tears when she came to collect Daphne's things."

"I expect she'll sell everything she can, and that'll be the last time she ever thinks of her mother. It's so sad when family relationships break down. We must never get like that."

"That would be impossible." I wrapped an arm around Gran's shoulders and squeezed. I couldn't imagine us having a bad relationship. "Kate mentioned Daphne had an eye for the guys. She said she was playing around behind Reggie's back."

A smile flickered across Gran's face. "Most likely. She could never resist a charming smile and a handsome face. She was a goer, despite getting on in years."

"Do you know if she had a fling with Pearl's guitarist, Jed?"

Gran snorted a laugh. "That wouldn't surprise me one bit. Daphne had a thing for rockers because they had excellent rhythm between the sheets."

I grimaced and held up a hand. "That's too much information. I saw Jed during the wedding reception, and he'd been with someone. Maybe it was Daphne."

"You'll have to ask Jed about that, but he fits her type."

"Is he easy to talk to?"

"He's a lovely guy. A rogue, but there's nothing bad about him. He won't mind talking to you. They're packing their equipment up, so you don't want to wait too long before speaking to him."

"I'll get right on that." I smiled at her. "But this is good news for you and Alice. We now have another suspect to follow."

"Oh, Holly! Jed isn't a killer."

"I still need to talk to him. Daphne could have told him she was worried about Reggie or Kate. Or Jed could have a dark side. He came back for seconds with Daphne, got rebuffed and she tried to fight him off, so he hit her."

Gran finally relaxed into her seat. "Do you really think whoever killed Daphne wasn't after me?"

"You're safe. You do look similar, but whoever killed Daphne would have seen her face and known it wasn't you."

"I suppose you're right. I scared myself by thinking the worst, and I didn't want anything bad to happen to Ray."

"Wait! Is that the reason you kicked him out? You want to keep him safe?"

She nodded. "I'll do anything to keep that man away from harm. He's made me so happy since we got together. I don't want anything bad to happen to him."

"The only bad thing that's happened to him is his new bride has booted him out before you've even been on your honeymoon. You're overreacting."

"Perhaps I am, but maybe he should stay at his old place for now, just in case this is more than the ramblings of an old woman."

"Gran! You're a happily married couple with plenty of amazing years ahead of you. You shouldn't spend your first days as man and wife apart. Go and see Ray. Apologize for overreacting, and hope he'll come back."

Gran looked around the room. "Seeing the old crew from prison and talking about the good old days brought back memories, not all of them happy. And people hold grudges.

I was worried someone had learned I was getting married and wanted to ruin things."

"You think a secret nemesis from your past snuck into your wedding to kill you?"

"When you put it like that ..." Gran chuckled.

"I think it's much more likely Daphne got in over her head. Whether that was with Reggie, or Kate, or even Jed, there are plenty more motives out there for wanting her dead than you. Now, go put my expensive knives away, open the curtains, and go get your husband back."

She gave me a tight hug. "You're right. But how are things with you? I haven't seen you since you went for breakfast with Rupert's parents. I'm sure they've fallen completely in love with you."

"Um, it's a work in progress. I'll need to do more before they accept me into the family."

"They're fools if they don't welcome you with open arms. Do you want me to have a word? I can tell them all your good points, and how Rupert is lucky to have you."

The last thing I needed was Gran twisting their arms. "I'm sure it'll be fine. Don't worry about my love life, you focus on your own."

"I will. I need to find Ray and apologize for being paranoid. Will you join us for dinner?"

"No, I'm not sure what time I'm getting back, so I'll catch up with you in the morning. I need to speak to Jed, and see if he was the one having a fumble in the closet with Daphne, and if anything went wrong between them."

"I can't see him being involved, he's a decent guy, but be careful." Gran walked me to the door.

"I will. No worrying about people lurking in the shadows trying to get you. I've got a list of suspects for Daphne's murder, and none of them are interested in you."

Gran kissed my cheek as she opened the door. "I'll make sure not to worry. Besides, I've got my new husband to lavish affection on. That'll keep me busy for the next few hours."

After I'd walked along the path, I turned back and looked at the apartment. A trickle of worry ran through me. I was certain Gran was wrong, but it wouldn't do any harm to keep an eye on her. I'd ask Saracen if he could spare one of his guys to take a walk past now and again. Although he'd have to be discreet. If Gran knew she was being spied on, she wouldn't be happy. But it was better to be safe than sorry.

Chapter 15

Quiet voices filtered out of the room my gran and Ray had held their wedding reception in. I entered it with Meatball, to find Jed standing with the drummer in the band.

I lifted a hand as I walked toward them. "You must be getting ready to go."

Jed nodded, his shoulder-length dark hair tied off his face in a man bun. "We don't usually pack up our equipment ourselves, but we've been hanging around all day waiting for the guy who usually does it. We got a message an hour ago that he's put his back out and can't move out of bed. So we got stuck lugging the stuff around."

"I'll get this monitor in the van." The drummer walked a large black case onto a set of trolley wheels and walked away.

"I thought you were great at my gran's reception," I said. "You had everyone up and dancing."

Jed grinned, revealing two deep cheek dimples. "That's always the plan. If the dancefloor isn't packed, we haven't won the night. It's such a shame it had to end early."

"Yes, it was a tragedy what happened to Daphne."

He sighed. "Yep. She was a fun lady."

"Did you know her well?" I followed him as he walked over to a small amp.

"Not really. I mean, she seemed like a lot of fun. I can't imagine why anyone would want to hurt her."

"My gran's really upset about it. She was close to Daphne."

"I'm sorry her wedding day was ruined," Jed said. "It shouldn't have happened. Do you know how the investigation is going?"

"There are a few suspects. Did you see much of Daphne at the reception?"

A grin flashed across his face but vanished as quickly as it arrived. "No, I was busy shredding the guitar on stage."

"So it wasn't Daphne you snuck into the closet to have fun with?"

His cheeks flushed pink, but he shook his head. "You must be thinking of someone else."

"Jed, maybe you've forgotten, but I saw you rolling out of the closet. The shade of lipstick you were wearing didn't suit you. It was much more Daphne's shade of pink."

He leaned against the raised stage. "Ah, darn it. I didn't want to say anything. It was our little secret. After all, I knew she'd come to the wedding with some other guy. A guy you don't want to mess with."

"So you were with Daphne for part of the evening?"

"She caught my eye as soon as I saw her. I always love confident women, and she had plenty of that. And she was good-looking. We got chatting at the bar and had a drink together, and she was flirting outrageously. It wasn't just me chasing after her, but I was happy to go along for the ride."

"Was this the first time you'd met?"

"No, I'd seen her around, but only to say hi to. She was friends with Pearl, and came to some gigs Pearl was involved in, but we'd never really talked like that before. I wish we had, we could have had a lot more fun together."

"Who suggested you go in the closet?"

He tilted his head from side to side, a roguish grin on his face. "We came to a mutual agreement."

"And what do you think of Daphne's date?"

Jed grimaced. "I kept out of his way. I could tell he wasn't a good guy. And I had to intervene when I heard them arguing outside. He told me to mind my business, but you should never raise your voice to a woman. I may not be as big as Reggie, but I can hold my own. When Reggie realized I wasn't backing down, he stormed off. I comforted Daphne to make sure she was okay, and then one thing led to another. She pretty much leaped on me and dragged me to the closet."

"Do you know what Reggie and Daphne were arguing about?"

"I didn't catch all of it, but it was something about another woman. Daphne wasn't happy."

"Do you think Reggie was cheating on her?"

"That's what it sounded like. I'm all for free love, so long as all parties approve, but if someone's not happy, you need to pump the brakes. Reggie sounded like he wanted to have his cake and eat it. You don't mess around on a woman like Daphne."

"How's everything going in here?" Pearl walked into the room. "Hello, Holly. It's nice to see you again. How's your gran doing? I want to drop in and see her before we leave."

"She'd like that. She's doing okay. I saw her a little while ago. How about you?"

"I'm making sure I keep myself busy," Pearl said. "I don't want to sit in the quiet for too long because I'll start crying. Daphne was such a dear friend. It was always the three of us against the world when we were inside. She was a tough nut."

"I was just talking to Holly about the fight Daphne had with Reggie," Jed said.

Pearl's top lip curled. "I hope the police have asked him lots of questions. I don't trust him. Never have."

"They are interested in him," I said. "And he doesn't have the best of alibis. Did either of you see him outside the castle around the time Daphne died?"

"No, we didn't see him, and we take our breaks outside. It gets hot under the lights when we're performing. We were out the back having a smoke when we heard the news about Daphne. I couldn't believe it," Pearl said.

"Reggie was supposed to be outside having a cigar," I said. "You're certain you didn't see him?"

"When Pearl says having a smoke, she means we were smoking some special ... herbal cigarettes I carry around. They take the edge off the nerves." Jed grinned. "This lifestyle is truly rock-and-roll."

"Ignore him. You don't need to hear about our wayward behavior," Pearl said. "Maybe some of the evening is hazy because of the ... herbs, but I'd have remembered seeing Reggie. He's hard to miss. And I can't stand the stench of cigar smoke, so if anyone had been out there smoking one, I'd have known. Do the police think he killed Daphne?"

"I'm wondering about his involvement," I said. "Daphne wasn't happy with him, and he has a temper. Those two things would be a bad mix."

"You be careful poking around in this," Pearl said. "You don't want your gran worrying about you."

"She knows what I'm like," I said with a smile.

"If we're talking suspects, though, I was wondering about Jane," Pearl said. "What did you think about her?"

"I didn't spend much time with Jane at the wedding," I said. "What makes you think she could be involved?"

"I don't know for certain she is, but Jane had a reputation when she worked at the prison."

"What kind of reputation?"

Pearl glanced around. "She was known as the fixer. She'd help you out if you got in trouble, or keep an eye on you if another inmate made a threat."

"Isn't that what prison guards are supposed to do?"

Pearl waggled her eyebrows. "Yes, you'd think that was in the job description, but Jane had a habit of turning a blind eye if she was given the right incentive. We all knew her secret, and all used her services when we got desperate. A prison guard's salary isn't spectacular, so she supplemented her income. Daphne would tease her about it all the time, and I saw them having a long conversation at the wedding."

"About what?"

"I didn't hear, but Jane didn't look happy. Maybe the police need to check Daphne didn't push her too far."

I glanced over at Jed, who was moving a large piece of equipment.

Pearl followed my gaze, and she smiled. "I take it you heard about Jed and Daphne?"

I nodded. "I did think they may have argued."

"If you're concerned that Jed had anything to do with it, don't be. He's a clean living vegan rocker these days. He wouldn't hurt a fly."

"Clean living apart from the alcohol and special herbal cigarettes?"

"Well, we all have different definitions of what clean means, but he was a wild one back in the day, and he still has an eye for the ladies.

I told him to keep his hands off Daphne when I found out they'd been messing around. If Reggie discovered what he'd been up to, he'd break Jed's fingers so he'd never play his guitar again. Jed soon backed off. He's a lover, not a fighter."

"Thanks. I just wanted to check." I smiled at Pearl. "When are you going?"

"We were hoping to leave this evening, but it's getting late, and I hate night driving. It's all our roadie's fault. If he'd bothered to let us know he'd put his back out bending over to tie a shoelace, we'd have figured something else out."

"Are you staying here another night?"

"Yes, and I won't mind another night of luxury before we leave. And it'll give me more time to go see your gran."

"I hope you get the chance. She'd appreciate the company." I felt bad leaving Gran, but she had Ray looking out for her, and I had to keep focused on solving this murder. "I'd better get going. I hope to see you before you leave."

"I'm sure you will." Pearl waved a hand at Jed. "Bend your knees, or you'll put your back out, too. Men, they always think they know best." She hurried off to chastise him.

I left them to their packing. After that conversation, I could rule out Jed, since he had Pearl and the drummer as his alibi. And it sounded like things had been friendly between him and Daphne after they'd had their fun. But I wouldn't mind a chat with Jane. Maybe there was something to the bent prison guard theory. If she needed to have her secrets kept, she could have seen Daphne as a threat and silenced her.

Chapter 16

I was up early after a restless night, all thanks to the suspects in Daphne's murder spinning through my mind.

I sat on the edge of my bed and sent a message to Saracen. If you'd like a free breakfast, head over to my apartment. We can talk suspects while we eat.

The response was almost instantaneous. I'm on my way.

I grinned as I hurried into the bathroom. Saracen could always be swayed by the promise of a good meal.

Twenty minutes later, I was showered, dressed, and standing at the stove when there was a knock at the door.

"I'll get that." Gran hurried to the door in her dressing gown. "That'll be Ray. He's probably forgotten his key."

"No, Gran, that's not Ray, it's—" I was too late as she yanked open the door.

Saracen's eyes widened as he stared at her frilly leopard print robe. He looked away, his cheeks pink. "Sorry to disturb you. Holly said it was okay if I came for breakfast."

"Come in. There's no need to be shy. I expect you're here to talk about Daphne." Gran ushered him into the kitchen.

Saracen nodded. "I didn't mean to get you out of bed."

"You didn't. Take a seat. I'll make the coffee." Gran bustled around the kitchen, not seeming to notice Saracen's embarrassment.

"I've made omelettes to keep us full," I said. "We've got a busy day ahead of us if we're going to figure out what happened to Daphne."

"Sounds good," Saracen said.

"Gran, you don't have to be here if you find it too difficult to talk about Daphne," I said.

"I insist on being here. She was my friend, and I want to help find out what happened, especially since my name could still be in the frame." Gran settled at the table after pouring coffee for everyone.

"You can relax on that front," Saracen said. "Now Princess Alice has made a run for it, the police are only interested in her. You're almost in the clear."

"Almost?" Gran tilted her head. "What makes them think I could be guilty?"

I studied him discreetly as I sautéed mushrooms. Did he know about Gran slipping out of the reception and not having an alibi?

"Your record," Saracen said.

Gran tutted. "My days as a criminal are in the distant past."

I cleared my throat and gave her a pointed look. The second she'd arrived in Audley St. Mary, she'd done a little pilfering.

She chuckled. "They are now. I'm not going to spoil all the wonderful things I've got in my life by killing someone."

Saracen's phone buzzed, and he checked it. "How long will breakfast be?"

"A few minutes," I said. "You can take that if you need to."

He hopped up and headed to the door. "Thanks. I won't be long."

The second he shut the door, I pointed my spatula at Gran. "I've been meaning to ask you, why didn't you say anything about changing your shoes?"

"My shoes?"

"You didn't tell Saracen you weren't at your wedding reception when Daphne died. You went off to get different shoes."

"Holly! What are you suggesting?"

"Nothing bad about you, but I'm thinking like a suspicious police officer looking at your record. If they learn you ducked out and kept quiet about it, it'll look bad."

She lined up the condiments on the table. "Which is exactly why I said nothing. And if you think I'm the killer, you could have told on me."

"Gran, I know you didn't do it, but maybe let Saracen know, so it doesn't come back to bite you."

I finished cooking the last omelette, took the warmed plates from the oven, and served up just as Saracen returned.

He grinned. "Perfect timing."

Gran had toast and marmalade, and I gave Saracen an extra helping of mushrooms and grilled tomatoes so he wouldn't feel left out by not having sugary carbs.

We spent a minute enjoying the breakfast before I set down my knife and fork. I nudged Gran.

She sighed. "Saracen, I have a confession to make."

His eyes widened. "About Daphne's murder?"

"Yes, but it's not what you think. I left the reception around the time of Daphne's death, but only to change my shoes. I was gone maybe fifteen minutes. I couldn't dance in my heels all night." She glanced at me. "I only kept quiet about it because I thought the police might jump on it."

Saracen's forehead wrinkled. "I'm certain they would. Where were your other shoes?"

"In a bag in the powder room. I kept my cosmetics and clothes in there so I wouldn't need to come back here."

"That's good! We can check the cameras," Saracen said.

"Or you could believe what I'm telling you."

His cheeks colored again. "I do. Let's keep this between us for now. I don't have you on my suspect list, anymore."

"You were never on mine," I said.

Gran pursed her lips. "Not even right at the bottom? I had the opportunity to do it."

"No! Don't even joke about that." I took a bite of omelette. "It's better not to have secrets, though."

"Agreed. I appreciate you telling me, Molly," Saracen said.

Gran nodded as she bit into her toast.

"We need to run through our remaining suspects," I said.

"And we now know I'm definitely not one," Gran said.

"You're not. And neither is Alice, no matter how incriminating the scene looked," I said.

"I agree," Gran said.

"And I ruled Jed out after talking to him."

"What did he have to say for himself?" Saracen said.

"He admitted to having a fumble with Daphne, but it wasn't him. He was outside with Pearl and the drummer. They were relaxing in between sets when Daphne was killed."

Gran smiled and nodded. "I can imagine what they were up to. But that's good. They're all friends of mine, and I don't want them involved in this."

"Have you gotten a look at the CCTV to see what Daphne's daughter was up to when she was here?" I asked Saracen.

"I was coming to that," he said. "Kate checks out. She arrived just before nine. She was sitting in her car for ten minutes, most of that time on her phone, probably trying to get in touch with Daphne. Daphne came out, they had a short conversation, and then Kate roared away in her car. She left the grounds before Daphne was murdered."

"So we can rule out the unhappy daughter," I said.

"Who does that leave us with?" Gran said. "We have to find out who did this so Princess Alice can come back to the castle. This is her home."

"The obvious suspect from the beginning has always been Reggie," I said. "And having spoken to Pearl and Jed yesterday, they didn't see him outside when he said he was. I reckon he still did it."

"But we need proof," Saracen said. "Maybe no one noticed him when he was outside because he was standing in the shadows, or they were too drunk. You had a lot of booze at your wedding, Molly."

Gran smiled. "I aim to please."

"I want to talk to Jane," I said.

"My prison guard friend?" Gran said. "What's got you interested in her?"

"It's something Pearl said. She confirmed that Jane did you all favors when you were in prison. Do you think Daphne could have tried to exploit that?"

"Are we talking about a bent prison guard?" Saracen said.

"I wouldn't say she was bent. Jane was always flexible with the rules, but only when it suited her and she didn't think she'd get caught. She could be useful, but you never wanted to get on her wrong side. If you did, she'd make your life miserable. We all used her services when we were inside."

"Could Daphne have had some secret she was holding over Jane?" I said.

"Nothing comes to mind," Gran said. "And Jane's retired now, so she's no use to anyone."

"What if Jane had something Daphne wanted? Could she have been after her savings or her pension pot?"

"There's not much pension to be had from a career like that," Gran said. "But Jane hated anyone talking about what she did. It was always a condition of hers. She'd help, so long as you kept quiet. Daphne used to tease her about it. She said that one day, she'd write her memoir and have a chapter all about Jane. Jane would go bright red and tell her to be quiet."

"Did Daphne write an incriminating memoir about her time in prison?" Saracen said.

Gran roared with laughter. "No! She only liked to read the funnies in the paper. She was never into writing."

"I'd still like to speak to Jane," I said. "If nothing else, maybe she saw Reggie was up to no good, then we can focus on him and figure out how to get a confession."

"She's staying at the Audley Hotel," Gran said. "You'll find her there if you hurry. I doubt she'll be sticking around for much longer, though."

"I'd like to come with you but need to update Lord and Lady Audley about the progress we've made in locating Campbell and Princess Alice," Saracen said. "They're not happy they haven't been found."

"I'm happy! The longer they stay hidden, the more time it gives us to figure out what really happened." I stood to clear the empty plates, but Gran waved me away. "You cooked, I'll clean. Unless Saracen wants to do it."

His cheeks flushed. "Um, I really need to get going."

"Ignore her, she's only teasing," I said. "Have you heard anything from Campbell or Alice? Any clue where they could be hiding out?"

"Not a peep. Campbell will have emergency supplies set up in different outposts around the country, so they can stay hidden for months."

"We won't need months," I said. "I want to figure this out today. It feels like we're up against a countdown clock with Rupert's parents and their lawyer trying to make out Alice is unstable."

"I find it romantic," Gran said. "Campbell whisking Alice away to keep her safe."

"Or stupid," I said.

"The things we do for love," Gran said. "You'd better get a wiggle on if you want to speak to Jane. I know she's checking out today."

"I'd better go," I said. "I'll catch up with you both later."

I raced to the castle equipment store, borrowed one of the bikes with a wicker basket on the front so Meatball could ride with me, and set off to the center of Audley St. Mary where the hotel was located.

It was a warm day, but not too hot that I was sweating as I zoomed along the narrow lanes of the village.

I pulled up outside the hotel and secured the bike, making sure Meatball was happy in his basket and not able to escape, before heading inside.

After a quick check at reception, the receptionist called up to Jane's room.

"She'll be down in a few minutes," she said.

"Great. I'll wait for her." I peeked out the window at Meatball, who was sitting with his front paws resting on the edge of the basket, watching the world go by.

Jane emerged from the elevator and strode over. "Holly, you wanted to speak to me." She wore a gray suit that wouldn't have gone amiss inside the prison she once worked in.

"Yes, have you got time for a cup of tea?"

"No. I'm leaving soon. What can I do for you?"

Straight to the point. I appreciated that. "It's about what happened to Daphne."

Jane gave a sharp nod. "That was a terrible business. I'm sorry for your gran. How's she holding up?"

"She'll be fine, but I know she'll feel better once the killer has been caught."

"Of course." Jane arched an eyebrow, waiting for me to go on.

I cleared my throat. "Can I ask you a couple of questions about the night of Daphne's murder?"

"Sure. What do you want to know?"

"I've heard you used to help the ladies when they needed things."

Her eyes narrowed a fraction. "Things?"

"When they were inside. Things that might have been considered contraband."

"Ah! That was a while ago. And of course, I helped the inmates. It was a low security prison, and they weren't there for serious crimes. Although now and again, your gran skated close to the line. So did Daphne, for that matter. But I wanted to see them reformed. Everyone deserves a second chance."

"What did you think of Daphne?" I said.

"She wasn't your model inmate."

"Did she ever cause you problems?"

"Now and again."

"Such as ..."

"Daphne didn't know when to keep quiet. That could get her in trouble, and not just with me, but with other inmates. She liked to sass people, and that wasn't always appreciated."

"Did she ever sass you?"

"Of course. But I liked Daphne and wanted her to do well for herself. She was a clever woman and knew how to play the game."

"The game?"

"Surviving inside. Not everyone takes to it." Jane tilted her head. "What's with these questions? I figured this was resolved. The police are pursuing the prime suspect. And it won't be long before they locate a person with such a high public profile, not with the crazy world of social media we live in. Someone will take a snap of Princess Alice, then the chase will be over."

"I'm not certain they've got things right," I said. "And Princess Alice is a friend of mine. I can't believe she'd do such a thing."

"Sometimes, your closest friends hide the darkest secrets," Jane said.

"It sounds like you've got experience of that."

She simply shrugged.

"The police have also been looking into Reggie, Daphne's boyfriend," I said.

"That's hardly a surprise, given his past."

"Did you see him during the wedding reception?"

"I did. I didn't pay him much attention, but when you've been in the business as long as me, you get an eye for the unsavory types. Reggie Frasier is definitely that."

"Do you think he's capable of murder?"

"He's not only capable, but he's committed such a crime on numerous occasions. And since you're asking about Daphne's associations, you must know about his criminal past. He's a bad seed, and she should have gotten rid of him a long time ago."

"Daphne was thinking about it. I wondered if Reggie had learned of her plans and wasn't happy about it."

"I couldn't tell you about that. We didn't have that kind of friendship. I'm not one for girly chats about guys."

"Where were you when you heard what happened to Daphne?"

Jane's mouth quirked up on one side. "I see where this is heading. You think I had something to do with her murder?"

"Not really, but you could have seen something odd. Maybe you even saw the killer leaving the castle but didn't realize it. Any clue could help us figure out what happened."

"I've told the police everything. I was outside the castle having a walk around. The band had stopped playing, and I wanted some air."

"Did you see Reggie out there?"

"He wasn't about, but the castle grounds are vast. We could have been on opposite sides of the castle. I was wandering around, looking at how the other half lives. I didn't see Reggie. I didn't see anyone I knew. I was about to head back inside, when several people rushed out and said the police were on their way because someone had been killed."

"Were you on your own?"

"I was. I didn't bring a date." Jane crossed her arms over her chest. "I had no problem with Daphne. We had our differences, but I respected her. She worked hard and took her opportunity to learn new skills. Those are the women I always think will do well when they get out, when they don't rest on their laurels and work to improve themselves. Daphne, Pearl, and your gran were much the same. That's when they weren't causing trouble when they got together."

"Do you think it likely Reggie killed Daphne?" I said.

"If it's not the runaway princess, then I'd go for him. Although ..." Jane looked around. "Have you spoken to Daphne's daughter?"

"Kate, yes. Why do you ask about her?"

"There was always trouble when she visited. She even once asked if Daphne's parole could be denied because she didn't want her living in the same house as her."

The more I got to know about Kate, the less I liked her, even though she had her reasons for being so cold to her mother.

"She's been spoken to and ruled out. She was at the castle that night but couldn't have done it."

"That's a pity. I'd have liked her to experience the inside of a cage, so to speak. She may have been more sympathetic to her mother if she knew that life inside wasn't always easy." Jane checked her watch. "Are we done? I need to get back to my room and finish packing. I've got a cab coming."

"Of course. Thanks." We said our goodbyes, and I headed outside to the bike. I petted Meatball on the head and then pushed away.

It would be easy to check Jane's alibi. There was a decent set of cameras around parts of the castle grounds, so if she'd been wandering around at the time of Daphne's death, she'd have been seen.

I sped around the corner and took my feet off the pedals, my hair flying behind me as I picked up speed downhill. Everything passed by in a blur.

The bike was just feeling out of control as I hit a bend and shot around it.

I squeaked and slammed on the brakes as someone stepped into my path. I almost pitched off the bike, making sure to grab Meatball so he was safe.

I turned and blew out a breath. "Rupert! I could have killed you."

He dashed over, a startled look on his face. "Holly, I'm so sorry. I was rather taken with this new book of poetry and wasn't looking where I was going. I didn't mean to scare you."

I turned the bike and wheeled back to him before pulling it up onto the verge. "You're lucky I'm so good on two wheels."

He smiled down at me. "You know, this reminds me of the very first time you whacked me with your bike."

"I knocked you out! People thought I'd killed you. And I thought I'd be out of a job when you came to because you'd be so angry with me."

His smile was affectionate as he looked down at me. "Your place at the castle is always safe. And I hope it becomes a permanent position for you, if you agree to be my wife."

"Um, about that. I made a terrible impression on your parents when we had breakfast."

Rupert tilted his head from side to side. "Maybe it wasn't the best impression, but you were distracted because you wanted to help Alice, I did tell them that."

"What was their response?"

He gave a slight shake of his head. "Give them time. They don't like change."

Which was his polite way of saying they hated me.

"But good news," Rupert said. "They've invited you to dinner tonight. I'm sure we can mend bridges, and they'll see how wonderful you are."

"No! I can't do that. Not now."

He caught hold of my hand. "Holly, this is important."

"More important than making sure your sister is innocent?"

"Oh, you know I don't mean that. Of course, I want to make sure everything is fine with Alice. And it will be. It's being sorted."

"No, it's not. Not if your parents have anything to do with it. Do you know what they have planned for Alice?"

Rupert lowered his gaze. "I do. They're worried she's not well."

"Alice is as healthy as an ox! You know that."

"I'm sure it's just something they're considering as a backup plan if the police decide to charge her."

"When I've heard them talking, it sounds like their only plan. I tried to protect Alice, but they wouldn't listen to me. They've got your fancy lawyer working on a case to show she isn't of sound mind. How will she feel when she hears about that? I can't think about having dinner with your parents when I have to focus on finding Daphne's killer."

"What about us?"

I shook my hand out of his grasp. "Maybe there shouldn't be an us." Everything felt overwhelming. My family, Alice included, were vulnerable, and Rupert's parents were making this too complicated.

The pained expression on his face lanced into my heart. "Don't say that. I love having you in my life. I don't want you to leave me."

"I should. Your parents don't like me. I'm wrong for you." I grabbed the bike handles and went to push it away. I needed space from Rupert. I couldn't let our relationship distract me from keeping Alice safe.

"Please, come to dinner with us tonight. I'll speak to my parents again and make them see sense."

"No, there won't be any dinner. Not now, or ever. I'm sorry. I can't do this." I hopped on the bike and dashed away, my eyes filling with tears. I did love Rupert, even though I'd never told him, but I'd never fit in with the Audley family.

All along, this had been a silly fantasy, and that had to end so I could focus on helping my friend. That's what I did best, helping others. Even if it sometimes hurt me to do that.

Chapter 17

"Do you know that's your fifth brownie?" Saracen looked at me from across the table in his apartment, an envious look in his eye.

"I didn't know you were keeping count." I popped the brownie bite into my mouth and chewed.

I'd found Saracen after speaking to Jane and following my spectacularly unsuccessful talk with Rupert. The talk where I'd ended our relationship. Crushed it at the first hurdle we'd faced like a coward.

Saracen shrugged and took a bite of the homemade low sugar muffin I'd brought with me. We'd spent a few hours going back over the suspects in Daphne's murder, all without success. And we still had no way to prove Reggie was the killer.

"That's number six," Saracen muttered.

I hadn't even realized I'd picked up another piece of brownie. I was comfort eating, stuffing down my sadness about my fight with Rupert. But it was better if we separated now, before we became even more entangled. I'd been right to say I was a bad match for him. His parents would never accept me, so it would always be awkward when we were together at family events.

"I, um, I'm not good at all the girly stuff." Saracen waved a hand in the air.

I slid him a glance. "What girly stuff are we talking about? Are you having problems with a woman?"

"No! I mean, I figured you'd usually talk to Princess Alice about, you know, girly stuff."

"I talk to Alice about lots of things, not just frilly dresses and lip gloss."

His cheeks flushed. "It's just, you don't seem happy. And you mentioned seeing Lord Rupert when you were coming back from the hotel. Did something happen between you?"

"Oh! That kind of girly stuff." I shook my head. "I don't want to talk about it."

Saracen was quiet for a moment. "Women always say that when they really do want to talk about something. Or so I've heard."

"Is that right? Are you sure you want to counsel me about my relationship with Rupert?"

He shuffled in his seat. "No, but maybe I can help you fix things. I'm great at fixing things."

"You're great at fixing engines, or working out the best route when you're hunting down a terrorist in the dead of night. I don't know if you can do anything to sort out what's going on between me and Rupert. I'm not even sure anything is going on. I stamped my foot right on our relationship. He's got every right not to forgive me, not that I'm sure he wants to forgive me. He was probably relieved when I said I wouldn't go to dinner with his parents and didn't fit in. I always knew we were an odd match. Meeting his parents confirmed that."

"So that's what happened," Saracen said. "You fought about his parents not accepting you?"

I chewed on the brownie. "Something like that. Like I said, I don't want to talk about it."

There was a knock on the apartment door. Saracen stood and opened it. "Lady Philippa!"

She bustled in, wrapped in a long dark green velvet coat, two matching feathers sticking out of her hair. "I've just had a distressing conversation with the police. They're still looking for Alice."

"Take a seat, Lady Philippa," Saracen said. "Can I get you something to drink?"

"I'll have tea and some of those brownies." Lady Philippa settled into the seat Saracen had pulled out for her. "I need to know what's going on. I can't get any sense out of the rest of the family. They keep treating me like I'm made of glass and will break if I hear bad news. I must know everything. Even if it's bad."

I glanced at Saracen. "I'll give you a quick update. No one knows where Alice or Campbell are."

"Which is good news," Lady Philippa said. "But I'm still worried. I keep sensing danger."

"Do you think they're in danger?" I said.

"That's just it, I can't be certain where the danger is focused. It makes sense Alice must be the one at risk because she's so vulnerable, and everyone's looking for her."

"You're sensing she's close to being caught?" I said.

Lady Philippa accepted the tea from Saracen, who then sat beside her. "No, nothing is clear about Alice's future. I keep seeing different paths for her. It's changing all the time."

"It's just bad dreams, Lady Philippa," Saracen said. "I know you're worried, but don't make yourself stressed. We still have suspects we're looking into. When we find the killer, we can get Princess Alice home."

"Tell me about the suspects. That may help me clear my thoughts."

"We've discounted almost everyone," I said. "They've all got alibis. Saracen has just been looking at the CCTV recordings from outside the castle on the night of Daphne's death to discount another suspect."

"Who are you looking for?" Lady Philippa asked.

"Jane Napoleon. She used to be a prison guard. Gran stayed in touch with her when she got out. We haven't found out where she was at the time of the murder."

"I'll keep looking while you're here. We can't rule out Jane just yet. She could still be involved." Saracen focused his attention on the laptop in front of him. "Although she has no criminal record, and nothing unusual is coming up on the searches I've run. She's a long shot at best."

"I wondered about Daphne's daughter. They had a bad relationship, but she was seen waiting outside the castle and left before Daphne was killed," I said.

"Who do you think killed Daphne?" Lady Philippa said.

"Her boyfriend, Reggie Frasier," I said. "He claims to have been outside smoking when Daphne was killed, but no one can say for sure where he was."

"So far, I've not seen him on the CCTV," Saracen said. "But look, I've just found Jane. She was outside around the time the murder happened."

We crowded around Saracen and watched some black and white footage for a few minutes. It showed Jane wandering around, sipping a drink.

"So we're back to Reggie," I said. "It has to be him."

Lady Philippa pressed her fingers to her forehead. "I'm not getting a male energy for this murder."

Saracen stared at Lady Philippa, then looked at me and lifted his shoulders.

I raised a hand to warn him off of questioning Lady Philippa's comment. "Do you think a woman killed Daphne?"

"I do. But everything feels muddled. It's as if something went wrong and it wasn't meant to happen that way."

"A dead body would be considered a successful outcome if you're trying to kill someone," Saracen said.

My phone buzzed on the table. It was Rupert calling again. It was the fifth call he'd made since we'd spoken, and I hadn't answered a single one.

Lady Philippa peered at my phone screen. "Aren't you going to speak to him?"

"No, I'm sure it's nothing important, and I have to focus on Alice."

"Hmmm, are you the danger I'm sensing?" Lady Philippa pursed her lips, her intense gaze leveled on me.

"I'm not a danger to anyone," I said.

"It feels like your relationship with Rupert is in danger. What happened between you?"

"They had a fight," Saracen muttered. "Holly's been comfort eating."

"It's nothing. We've realized we're wrong for each other." My heart hurt when I said those words. I looked at the almost empty tray of brownies and my stomach gave an unhappy grumble.

"I've never met a pair more right for each other," Lady Philippa said. "What's got you doubting your affections?"

"Possibly the worst introduction to my future in-laws I could have dreamt up," I said. "And I hate what they're trying to do to Alice."

Lady Philippa lifted her chin. "I heard they've got Peterson looking into a diminished responsibility plea."

I nodded. "They aren't even trying to defend her. They've written Alice off as crazy before she's told her side of the story."

Lady Philippa sighed. "I feel guilty. I had a nice plain-clothed policeman and a psychologist visit me today. They talked for almost an hour about my health and if I'd ever had dark thoughts or desires to harm people."

I whacked my hand on the table. "They're looking for a family history of mental instability. It'll be used as evidence against Alice so they can shut this case quickly and send her away."

Saracen kicked me under the table. "Holly! Lady Philippa is very mentally stable."

Lady Philippa waved away his comment. "I'm as kooky as they come, and proud of it, but I know what people think about me, and I don't care. I see much more than they do, and my life is better for it. The family is scared. They don't understand Alice and her free spirit, and they're trying to keep her safe."

"They should believe their own daughter," I said. "If they knew her at all, they'd know she wasn't capable of something like this. Alice doesn't even squash bugs."

"We know that," Lady Philippa said. "But her parents are cautious of her. They probably see this as the least worst option for Alice right now."

"Well, I don't, and I'm not afraid to tell them that," I said. "And that means I can't be with Rupert. I won't keep my mouth closed about this problem when I'm around them, and that means they're never going to like me."

"You're giving up on love because of one little roadblock?" Lady Philippa said.

"It seems like a huge roadblock to me. I feel like I'm having to make Rupert choose between them or me, and I don't want that. I don't want to separate Rupert from his parents."

Lady Philippa patted my hand. "You shouldn't worry about that. His parents separated themselves from him and Alice a long time ago. They did what they needed to provide an heir for the family fortune and then got on with the business of being an Audley. They were never warm, loving parents. They believe in duty before anything else. I was concerned about Alice and Rupert's well-being until they moved here. Then everything changed."

"I'm glad the Duke and Duchess opened their home to them."

"Why not? It's not as if we don't have the space. And they've been a joy to have living here." Lady Philippa smoothed a hand down my hair. "You won't have to deal with them often. This is the first time in a long time they've been to visit. If you can put up with the occasional formal visit, that's all you'll have to do."

I wrinkled my nose. The occasional visit when Rupert's parents would make it clear I was a bad fit. And what about when children arrived? Would they try to force their own sterile, formal values on them? Lady Audley had already mentioned boarding school. It didn't bear thinking about.

"It's not uncommon for people not to get on with their in-laws," Saracen said. "Lord Rupert is into you. Maybe you can put up with his parents if you only have to see them once a year."

"It still doesn't feel right," I said.

"You never give up on something so easily," Lady Philippa said. "You're scared. You're letting your fear of change hold you back from happiness. Rupert would make you very happy. You know that."

I let out a sigh. I did care for Rupert, but I wasn't sure it was enough.

"Let's focus on Reggie for now," I said. "We need to find a way to get him to crack, then we can bring Alice and Campbell home."

"You're only putting off the inevitable," Lady Philippa said. "You're going to have to fix things with Rupert soon enough."

"I will." As soon as I figured out how to.

"So, what are you going to do about Reggie?" Lady Philippa said.

"I've got my guys keeping an eye on him," Saracen said. "He's in the village at the moment having a few drinks. Once he gets back, we'll bring him in for questioning."

"Will that be enough? How will you get him to confess?" I said.

"We'll lay it all out for Reggie, show him all the other suspects have alibis, or have been discounted, and he's the only one left standing. And he lied about being outside when Daphne was killed. That may get him sweating, so he makes a mistake."

"He knows Alice is on the run. He'll think he's got nothing to worry about." I wasn't a hundred percent convinced by this plan. It wouldn't be the first time Reggie had locked horns with the police, and he'd be difficult to break.

"Campbell's taught me well when it comes to getting information out of people."

Lady Philippa gasped. "You'll use torture?"

He snorted a laugh before composing himself. "No, not torture. Nothing illegal."

"Can I be in on the questioning?" I said.

Saracen shook his head. "We're working together, but even I know when to draw the line. Reggie's a dangerous guy, and you've already tangled with him once. You don't want to push your luck. Leave this to me, I'll get him to crack."

"I want to do something helpful. I can't just sit here," I said.

"How about you take Lady Philippa back to her room and make sure she's comfortable?" Saracen said.

I frowned. That wasn't what I had in mind.

"I could do with a nap," Lady Philippa said. "Maybe I'll have another dream and learn the reason I'm so worried. I wish this horrible feeling would go away. I want everything to go back to normal. I want Alice and Campbell home, and I want Rupert and Holly back together."

My stomach cramped, and I couldn't decide if it was my gut pinging me a warning about this situation, or the fact I'd eaten way too many brownies.

"Come on, Lady Philippa, let's get you back to the turret. With a bit of luck, this will all be over soon," I said.

"Yes, then we can start planning your wedding." Lady Philippa stood.

I simply nodded, not wanting to dash her hopes. The chances of me and Rupert getting our happily ever after were a dim, unrealistic possibility. A dim possibility I was still avoiding facing.

Chapter 18

A new morning brought a thudding on the front door of my apartment, dragging me from a restless sleep. I rolled out of bed and grabbed my robe as I hurried to the door.

"What's all this noise?" Gran hurried out of her room, her hair mussed as she rubbed her eyes.

"I'm not sure." I pulled open the door to find Saracen outside.

"Reggie's done a runner." He stepped inside, his expression tight as he ran a hand across his hair.

I blinked the sleep out of my eyes. "What happened?"

"He came back to the castle last night, and I questioned him. I must have grilled the guy for over an hour, but he said nothing to incriminate himself. He just kept saying he was outside when Daphne died. We even found a cigar stub he claimed was his in a stone urn. He said that was proof he was where he said he was."

"Sit down, both of you. This calls for strong coffee." Gran ushered us to the table in the kitchen and started brewing coffee.

"He mentioned the cigar to me, too," I said. "But if he's innocent, why is he on the run?"

"Because he's not innocent," Saracen said. "He knows we're onto him. He did this. He killed Daphne."

I nodded. "I agree. How long has he been gone?"

"I finished talking to him about nine o'clock last night, and then he went up to the guest wing. I could tell he wasn't happy, but I couldn't charge him with Daphne's murder, and I didn't even have enough evidence to hold him. I've let the police know what's going on, but they're not interested. They're still focused on Princess Alice. They think it was her."

"Of course they are," I said. "Who saw Reggie leave the castle?"

"No one. He snuck out during the night. He cleared his room and must have walked out of the grounds. No cars were recorded on the cameras."

"Typical Reggie," Gran said. "He's always been as slippery as an oiled-up eel."

"We have to stop him," I said.

"We're working on it. I've got a team scouring the village and looking over the CCTV. We've also linked in with the police to see if we can get a look at public transport cameras to see if Reggie got on a bus or a train." Saracen accepted a mug of coffee from Gran, who joined us at the table.

"What kind of head start does he have?" I said.

Saracen grimaced. "At the most, nine-hours."

I groaned. "He could have left the country by now. We're too late. We'll never be able to prove he murdered Daphne."

"We will. It's not over yet."

"If I ever get my hands on Reggie, I'll strangle him for what he's done to Daphne," Gran said. "She deserved so much better."

"You need to stay away from him," I said. "There's nothing good about Reggie, and I don't want him hurting you."

She huffed out an angry breath. "I'd like to see him try."

"I need to get back." Saracen downed his coffee. "I just wanted you to know what's going on. We will get Reggie."

"Thanks, Saracen. I appreciate that," I said.

He'd just reached the door when his phone rang, and he answered the call. He turned to me, his eyes wide. "Where was that? Okay, I'm on my way."

"Have they caught Reggie?" I said.

Saracen scrubbed at his forehead. "Bad news. Alice and Campbell have been spotted, and the police are closing in on them."

My stomach flipped. "No! If they catch them, it's all over for Alice."

"And Campbell," Saracen said.

"Where are they? Maybe we can get to them before the police and help them hide," I said.

"They're about ninety miles from here in Banbury."

"I'm surprised they didn't leave the country," Gran said.

"Campbell must have hoped the killer would be found quickly," I said. "We've let them down on that front."

"They may still get away," Saracen said. "Campbell's good at what he does."

"But they can't keep running. Send me their exact location." I was already heading to my bedroom to pull on some clothes. I wasn't letting Alice and Campbell get caught. There had to be something I could do to help.

"Sure, but there's no way you can get to them in time, not unless you have a hypersonic jet," Saracen said from the kitchen.

"Not a jet, but I know one way I can get to them fast, but I'll need help to do it," I yelled from my bedroom.

"You should go, Holly," Gran called out. "Make sure Alice and Campbell are safe. Alice will need a friend."

"It's a bad idea," Saracen said. "You'll get in trouble with the police if they catch you interfering."

I returned to the kitchen. "Then I'll get in trouble. I'm not letting Alice and Campbell take the fall for this. We have to convince the police of Reggie's guilt."

Saracen sighed, but then took out his phone. "I've sent you the coordinates of their last known sighting."

"Great. That's a start. You liaise with your team and keep me up to date with Alice and Campbell's movements. I need to make a call."

Saracen nodded, then raced out the door.

I bit my lip as the number rang. It was early, and I wasn't certain Rupert would be awake. I let it ring for as long as possible, and was just about to hang up, when it was answered.

"Holly! Sorry, I was asleep. I've been trying to reach you since yesterday. I—"

"Rupert, I need your help. Alice and Campbell have been spotted by the police. We need to get to them. We have to make sure they aren't arrested."

There was silence for several long heartbeats. "Of course. What do you need from me?"

"I need to use the helicopter. It's the only way we can get there quickly enough."

"I'll call our pilot. How soon do you need to go?"

"Five minutes ago, but as quickly as possible."

"He lives locally. He can get here in fifteen minutes."

"Tell him to hurry. I don't know how long Campbell can keep evading the police."

"Leave it to me. I'll meet you at the helipad in ten minutes."

"Thanks, Rupert." I ended the call and stared at the phone. There was so much I wanted to say to him, but now wasn't the right time. I could always depend on Rupert, and that meant a lot in a relationship.

I raced out of my room and almost slammed into Gran.

She thrust a mug of coffee into my hand. "Drink this and take a few deep breaths."

"I don't have time. Rupert's getting the helicopter ready so we can fly to Banbury. We may still have a chance to help."

"You'll save them, you always do. But I insist you have something to drink and eat before you go."

There was no point in protesting, so I slugged back the coffee, choking at the alcoholic taste that burned down my throat. "Gran! What's in this?"

"A super boost. I always use whiskey when I'm under stress. It gets the gears going. Drink it down and then take these scones. You can eat them on the journey."

I managed a few more sips of coffee, but it was too strong for me to handle. "I've got to go." I kissed her on the cheek and grabbed the scones. "Meatball needs to stay with you. He's never flown in a helicopter, and I don't want him getting scared. I'll be back as soon as I can."

"Don't worry about us. Go save your friend," Gran said.

Although my stomach was churning, I munched on a scone as I jogged to the helipad in the castle grounds. I didn't want to eat, but I wasn't the greatest of flyers, and zooming around in a helicopter on an empty stomach would end in disaster of the sick bag kind.

I raised a hand as I saw Rupert waiting by the helicopter, and my heart did a somersault. I'd been mean to him yesterday and regretted it. Lady Philippa was right, I could handle an awkward annual meeting with his parents if it meant a lifetime of happiness. The discomfort would be worth it to spend the rest of my life with Rupert. And that's what I truly wanted, even if it was terrifying.

"Is the pilot on his way?" I said in the way of a greeting.

Rupert shook his head. "No, I contacted him, but he's down with food poisoning and can't fly."

My eyes widened as my stomach sank. "How will we get to Alice and Campbell? If we drive, it'll take too long."

He grinned. "I'm flying us."

My mouth dropped open. "You know how to fly a helicopter?"

"Sure. I've been flying for years."

"How did I not know this about you?"

His smile widened. "There are lots of things we don't know about each other, but if you give me time, we can find out all the fun stuff."

"Oh, Rupert!" I threw my arms around him and kissed him.

He smiled down at me. "I'm so sorry about pushing you yesterday. It means so much to me that everyone gets on, but I know that's not always possible."

I shook my head. "I'm sorry, too. I was being stubborn. I don't want to be without you. Rupert, I love you. We can work this out. But first, you need to get this thing off the ground so we can save our friends."

"My lady, your flying chariot awaits." He pulled open the door and helped me get inside.

I strapped in securely as he started the helicopter.

"Are you ready?" he said.

"Let's get out of here."

We took off and shot into the sky. I gave Rupert the directions, and he input them into the GPS. "We'll be there in thirty minutes."

I called Saracen and let him know we were on our way, before sitting back in my seat and trying to relax. The trees below us whizzed past, and my stomach wasn't all that happy. It was already a big bundle of nerves, and this jolting ride did me no favors.

Rupert squeezed my knee. "What made you change your mind? You seemed so sure things wouldn't work between us."

"I spoke to someone a lot wiser than me, and she made me see I could be too stubborn for my own good. I overreacted, and I'm a bit scared about our future. Your life is so different from mine, and I wasn't sure how I'd fit in."

"We both lead different lives, but we have the same values and ideals. We want to make the world a better place and ensure there's more good than bad in it. I think that's the perfect foundation for us to build on."

I'd have kissed him again, but needed to make sure he focused on his flying. "I agree. Now, if we can figure out this mess with your sister and Campbell, everything will be perfect."

My phone rang. It was Saracen. "They haven't been caught, have they?"

"No, they're still evading the police, but they're running out of time. I'm calling because Reggie's been spotted. He got on a train two hours ago. Holly, we're too late to stop him. He could have changed trains several times since then. Reggie could be anywhere by now."

My heart sank. With Reggie gone, we'd lost our prime suspect.

"The team's doing what they can, but it would have been easy for Reggie to get off at any one of a dozen stops and change his mode of transport," Saracen said.

"What about tracking his phone?"

"No such luck. Reggie uses burner phones and changes them regularly. We can't get him with that."

"He'll have to resurface eventually, then we'll nab him. In the meantime, we'll do what we can to make sure the police don't grab Alice and Campbell." We said our good-byes, and I ended the call.

"That didn't sound good," Rupert said.

"We're certain Reggie killed Daphne, and Saracen questioned him about it last night. Reggie must have gotten scared. He disappeared in the middle of the night, and no one knows where he is."

"Between you and Saracen, you'll find him again. You always stop the killer."

"That's the plan, but let's get to Alice first."

The next twenty minutes were a white-knuckle ride as Rupert pushed the helicopter to its limits.

He circled around, slowing the helicopter. "There are several police cars down there. We must be close."

"Can you land in that field?" I pointed to a public park below.

"Not officially, but since this is an emergency, I'll take us in. Hold on."

I gripped the handle on the door for dear life as we zoomed toward the ground, leaving my stomach somewhere among the clouds.

Rupert expertly landed the helicopter. He leaped out, helped me out, and we ran toward the police cars.

I pulled out my phone and tried Alice's number, but it was disconnected. "There must be a way we can reach them. Saracen has tried everything to get through to Campbell. Calls, messages, emails, he's not replying to a single thing."

We reached the police cars, and they were all empty.

"Maybe Campbell's got a hideout or a safe house around here," I said. "Where would you choose around here if you needed to keep a low profile?"

"I'm not sure. This is an average sized town, so it would be easy to blend in," Rupert said.

I did a slow turn, looking around. "I'd pick something on a quiet road with a back entrance. Something you could get in and out of without being overlooked."

There were several shouts, and I whirled around to see where they were coming from. My heart plummeted. The police were marching toward the cars, and they had Campbell handcuffed between them. Behind him, Alice was being led by a female police officer.

My hand flew to my mouth, and I gasped. We were too late. Reggie had escaped, and Alice and Campbell were captured. There was nothing I could do to help them.

Chapter 19

I paced the long main hall in the castle. It had been hours since Campbell and Alice had been arrested, and I'd not been able to speak to either of them. As soon as the police had seen me and Rupert lurking around their cars, they'd ushered us away. Alice and Campbell had been put in the back of separate police cars and driven away.

I'd never felt such defeat.

"Holly, you'll make a groove in the floor if you don't sit down." Saracen was perched on the edge of a high-backed wooden chair, his hands clasped together.

"There must be something we can do to help them," I said. "What's taking so long?"

"We're fortunate the police didn't put them straight in the cells," Saracen said. "We have Rupert's parents to thank for that."

"Of course. They want to make sure there isn't a public scandal by having their daughter dragged to a police station."

Saracen was quiet for a moment. "They're not bad people, and they're trying to do the right thing by Alice, but—"

"They failed her. So did I." I huffed out a breath. Lord and Lady Audley were so different from me. They had this high standing in the community that they didn't want damaged. It seemed to come before anything else. Right now I was too frustrated to focus on anything other than that my best friend was about to be charged with murder and declared insane, and the real killer was in the wind.

Rupert hurried along the corridor, Peterson beside him, his head bent as they talked to each other.

I hurried over to them. "What's going on? What's happening with Alice?"

Peterson glanced at Rupert. "We're making good progress."

"You can tell Holly everything," Rupert said.

Peterson lifted an eyebrow, then nodded. "I've been talking with Princess Alice, and we're making plans."

"What plans?" I said. "Can I see her yet? I expect she could use a friend."

"We're not letting anyone in to see her at the moment. She's resting. It's been a difficult time for her."

"Has she been charged yet?" I said.

"No formal charges will be brought at this time. I've recommended she have a psychological evaluation. Her mind is fragile considering the abduction she endured. It could have tipped her over the edge."

"Abduction? What are you talking about?" I said.

"Let me show you out, Peterson. Thanks for taking the time with my sister." Rupert led Peterson away, leaving me waiting for answers.

"Did you hear that?" I strode back to Saracen. "What are they talking about an abduction for?"

Saracen leaned his chin in his hands. "I can guess. Campbell's fallen on his sword to protect Princess Alice."

I turned at the sound of approaching footsteps to see Rupert returning. "Is this true? Is Campbell saying he abducted Alice?"

Rupert nodded. "He said he took her against her will."

I gasped in shock. "The police won't believe that. Why did he say he took her?"

"He's not saying much, other than that Alice had nothing to do with what happened. He forced her to leave the castle and then hid them away."

"Which is rubbish! Campbell doesn't have any reason for doing that," I said.

"Blackmail? Selling her to some dodgy gang? Slave trade? There are options if you go dark enough," Saracen said.

"Peterson thinks the police will buy one of those options," Rupert said. "And my parents much prefer the idea of an abduction case getting into the news than Alice being in the frame for murder."

I snorted my derision. "I imagine they do. You don't support this, do you?"

"I don't, but that's what Mother and Father are leading with. Campbell will be punished, and Alice will get away with murder by being declared mentally incompetent. She'll be sent away for treatment."

"Treatment she doesn't need." My hands clenched. This was so unfair on Alice and Campbell.

Rupert sighed. "We know that. But the police have enough evidence to charge Alice with manslaughter, at the very least. We can't let that happen."

"Does she still not remember what happened that night?" I said.

"Only Peterson and the doctor have been in to see her, so I'm uncertain. If she had anything useful to say, it hasn't gotten back to me."

"Campbell will go down for this," Saracen said. "All his previous good service will be forgotten, and he'll be labeled a kidnapper."

"We know why he's doing this," I said. "I need to speak to him and get him to see sense."

"There's a police guard outside the room they're using to hold him in," Rupert said. "No one gets in or out without their permission."

"Which room?" I said.

"The Tapestry room."

"Priest passages run past that room, I've been in them with Alice. Saracen, can you distract the police officer while I sneak in and talk to Campbell?"

"Sure, but what will you say to him?"

"I need him to reconsider what he's doing. It would break Alice's heart if he went to prison because he was helping her. She'd never forgive herself."

"If you're going to do it, you need to act quickly," Rupert said. "The police were talking about taking Campbell to the station to charge him. Once he's there, it'll be too late."

"Then let's move," I said. "Saracen, are you up for this?"

"Always. Campbell needs us. I'll cause a distraction while you sneak in."

"I need your help too, Rupert. I'm not sure how to access to the priest passage that runs past that room."

"No problem. I know the way in." Rupert took my hand as we hurried along the corridor, away from Saracen. "The entrance into the tunnel is behind this wall covering. Give me a minute to hunt it out." He slipped behind a large, multi-colored tapestry that hung against the stone wall.

After a few seconds of shuffling, I heard a small click.

"Got it," he said.

I checked to make sure the corridor was clear before slipping behind the wall covering with

Rupert. I could just see a dark passageway through the open door.

I kissed him on the cheek. "I won't be long. Keep an eye out to see if anyone comes this way. I don't want the police to find out what I'm doing."

"I'll cover for you," he said. "But hurry."

I pulled out my phone and used the flashlight function as I sped along the corridor. I counted my steps until I was certain I was in the right location to get into the room Campbell was being held.

I shone the flashlight over the rough stone and then slid my fingers into a narrow slot. The handle was stiff, but suddenly the door cracked open.

I pushed it wider, blinking at the bright light in the room.

Campbell stood in front of the door, his hands clenched as if he was about to attack.

"Stand down, it's just me." I snuck out of the door and pushed it shut behind me.

"Holly!" Campbell lowered his fists. "What are you doing?"

"I needed to see you. Are we okay to talk?"

"I'm on my own," he said. "There's a police officer outside the door, so keep your voice down. You're taking a risk by coming in here."

"It's a risk worth taking. What are you doing telling the police you kidnapped Alice?"

He cracked his jaw from side to side. "That's what I did. I took her against her will. Princess Alice is innocent."

"No, you helped her escape just before she was sent away to be evaluated by a psychologist and charged with manslaughter. You did a good thing. I'm proud of you."

"I'm not so sure about that." Campbell sank onto the couch and dropped his head into his hands. "We should have stayed. You told me it wasn't a good idea."

"I didn't have any better idea. And as soon as I heard what Alice's parents had planned for her, I realized we needed as much time as possible to get a confession from Reggie for Daphne's murder."

"You know it was Reggie?" Campbell lifted his head, hope glinting in his eyes.

"He doesn't have a decent alibi, he lied about where he was when Daphne was killed, and they were having relationship difficulties. We just need to find evidence to prove it was him."

"I heard he's disappeared," Campbell said.

"He's still missing. He got scared when Saracen questioned him. We should have been more discreet and gathered all the evidence before trying to get a confession."

He sighed. "Let me guess, the police have zero interest in tracking down Reggie now they have Alice and me back."

"Pretty much. But we're still looking for Reggie, and he can't stay hidden for long. He'll need access to money."

"No, he won't. A crook like Reggie will always be prepared. He'll have cash stashed in various locations and be able to survive on that for months. By then, it'll be too late for Alice. The damage will be done."

"I'm not ready to give up. How was Alice when you were with her?" I said. "Did she tell you anything useful about the night of the murder?"

"No, and at first, she was shaken by what was happening. We almost turned back half a dozen times. Princess Alice kept on saying she was worried she was guilty. I couldn't let her think that, so I needed to give her time to remember what happened."

"Nothing shifted? She didn't get her memories back?"

"No, although she was having flashes of memory recall and kept saying she was seeing your gran, which made no sense."

"It does make some sense. Daphne and Gran looked the same. Maybe that's what Alice is getting confused about."

"It doesn't really matter. It's not helping find evidence against Reggie."

"Maybe not, but I've been trying to figure out what caused Alice's memory loss. Could a drug have affected her?" I said.

"There are plenty of drugs that mess with short-term memory. But who'd want to drug her and set her up like this?"

"The doctor took a sample of Alice's blood the morning after the murder. Do you know what the results were? That could help to prove her innocence."

Campbell shook his head, frustration simmering just beneath the surface. "The police aren't telling me anything, and all Peterson said was that Alice is comfortable, and she's not in much distress."

"She shouldn't be in any distress," I said.

"This is all my fault. Now I can't do anything to help Alice."

"You can't, but I can. I'm still working with Saracen and the rest of your team to find out where Reggie is."

Campbell caught hold of my hand, and the sadness in his eyes made a lump form in my throat. "I'll do anything, whatever you want, just please find who killed Daphne. I can't bear Alice being treated like a lab rat and accused of something she didn't do."

"That won't happen. And if it does, I'll break her out of the psych ward myself and we'll go on the run. We'll Thelma and Louise it to safety."

A smirk crossed his face. "You do remember how that movie ended?"

"Oh! Okay, we won't drive off a cliff, but I'll make sure Alice gets free and her name is cleared, no matter how long it takes. All we need to do is find Reggie, get him back, and make him confess."

"That's no easy task with a crook like Reggie," Campbell said. "Are you absolutely sure it was him?"

"He's the only option left," I said. "The other suspects all have alibis."

Campbell nodded. "I wish I could help you catch him."

"You focus on helping yourself, and stop telling the police you kidnapped Alice. Saracen said you could go to prison for that."

"I don't care if it means Alice gets off the hook. She didn't run, she was forced to leave."

"No, she wasn't. Campbell, you love your work, and you don't want to go to prison."

"I can handle prison."

I shook my head. He was being unbelievably stubborn. "It won't come to that. I promise you, I'll clear Alice's name."

"Don't make promises you can't keep."

"I'll keep it. Even if I have to search for Reggie non-stop, I won't rest until he's caught. You need to look after yourself, though. If this goes wrong for Alice, she'll need all the friends she can get, especially since her parents have turned on her." I scowled. "Saracen said they're trying to do the right thing by her, but I don't see how anything is right about this."

Campbell swiped a hand down his face. "I've been around them a fair few times. They're traditional and have values they rigidly stick to. Upholding the family name and that kind of thing. It matters to them."

"It's like they're from another era. They don't see Rupert or Alice as separate people with their own ambitions, just pawns in the family name game."

"We'll never understand how these kinds of networks operate, not fully," Campbell said. "We're tangled up in them without knowing all the rules. You can't win when you play like that."

"I'm more than happy to break the rules I do understand, so long as Alice isn't mistreated." I glanced at the door. "Is there nothing I can do to convince you to change your mind about confessing to kidnapping Alice?"

"Not until you find Reggie. I'm sticking to my story. It's her only chance."

"Then I'll find him. On one condition."

Campbell lifted his head. "What's that?"

"When this is over, you tell Alice exactly how you feel about her."

"Not a chance. You're the one out of your mind if you think I'm doing that," he said.

"I'm serious, Campbell. You're this close to losing her. This close to having your life turned upside down, and all because you're protecting Alice. Your actions speak louder than any words, but sometimes, a person needs to hear those words. Alice needs to know you love her."

"I ... I never said I loved Princess Alice."

"But you do. You put up with her quirky ways, her unique outlook on life, and you're always there to protect her, even when it messes with your own life. And you know she adores you."

Color flushed on his cheeks as he glanced at me. "Even if what you said is true, it can't work between us."

"It's working for me and Rupert, and I thought it never would."

"Are you sure about that? I didn't think his parents liked you."

"Oh, they don't. But I'll barely see them. They're a small price to pay for happiness with Rupert."

Campbell was silent as he stared at the door. "You're right. I never want to lose Alice."

"Does that mean you'll tell her how you feel once I save you both from prison?"

He grunted. "I'll do it, providing you tell Rupert you love him."

"I've already beaten you on that. He knows. And despite his parents' lack of approval, we're going to be together."

"Darn it. I thought I had you. What convinced you to tell him?"

"I got over my fear. And you need to do the same."

"I'm not scared of anything."

"You're scared of Alice rejecting you."

"I'm … maybe I am." Campbell heaved out a sigh. "You've backed me into a corner. Okay, if you get me out of this mess, I'll tell Princess Alice exactly how I feel about her."

"I can't wait. But you may need to stop calling her Princess Alice if you date. It's kind of weird."

His smile was genuine as he shook his head. "She'll always be a princess to me. Now, get out of here and go find the killer, Holmes."

Chapter 20

The moon was high in the sky as I paced outside the castle with Saracen beside me. My head ached, my eyes felt strained, and the heavy weight of exhaustion felt like it was forcing my shoulders down.

"We're missing something," I said. "Reggie has to be out there somewhere."

We'd spent all day trying to find him, without success.

"He is, but he's using his criminal contacts to stay hidden. He'll have a network across this country that owes him favors. And he'll stay hidden until this all blows over," Saracen said.

"Or until Alice gets charged with killing Daphne," I said. "Any more news from the police on that front?"

"Nothing new. The police have been put off until tomorrow. But after the doctor's checked Alice over, she'll be questioned."

"I need to see her before then," I said. "Is there any chance you can get me in to her room?"

"She's under guard, just like Campbell was."

Campbell had been taken from the castle at lunch time. There was no news yet if he'd been charged with kidnapping Alice, but it was only a matter of time. I was hoping he was keeping quiet, so we had a few more hours to find Reggie.

"Alice isn't in isolation, though. She must be having her meals brought to her bedroom," I said.

"That's right. She's being allowed certain privileges while the police wait for her diagnosis to see if she's fit to stand trial," Saracen said.

"We can use that. I can take a supper tray to her."

He nodded. "That could work. I'll check to see who's guarding the room to make sure they won't recognize you."

"You do that, and I'll go to the kitchen and make up a tray of her favorite treats. Alice deserves them after all this. I'll meet you in the corridor in ten minutes."

We hurried off in opposite directions. I couldn't bear the thought of not seeing Alice again, and if I didn't get into her room tonight, it would be too late tomorrow morning. She'd be sent away under doctor's orders and monitored by the police.

The kitchen was quiet as I entered. I walked over to the large glass fronted refrigerator and scanned the contents. Alice loved anything sweet in a time of crisis.

I chose a slice of maple tart, a triple chocolate brownie, and a strawberry meringue. I set them out carefully on a tray, and then made a rich hot chocolate, decorating it with spray cream and chocolate sprinkles. That should cheer her up.

I left the kitchen and headed up the stairs to Alice's room. I was met by Saracen at the end of the corridor.

He gave me a thumbs up. "It's all good. It's one of the new police officers, so you won't be recognized. I said you were coming up with food, so you're expected."

"Thanks, Saracen. I can't wait to see Alice." I composed my face to hide my excited nerves and then headed to Alice's bedroom. I nodded at the police officer. "I'm bringing supper to Princess Alice."

He knocked on the door. "Food's here."

"I'm not hungry," her voice said from the other side of the door.

"I'll take it in, anyway," I said. "The princess may want it later, and I don't want to have to wait around for another demand. You know what these families are like, always expecting you to run around after them no matter how late it gets. And I want to put my feet up and watch some TV."

"You can go in, but I need to check what's on the tray." The police officer lifted the lids one by one. "There's a lot of dessert here."

"That's what Princess Alice likes to eat in the evenings." I bit my lip. Maybe there should have been more than sugar as a food group on this tray.

"Go in, but don't be too long." He pushed open the door.

I glanced down at Meatball. "Do you like dogs?"

He shrugged. "Sure. I had one when I was a kid."

"Can I leave Meatball with you?"

"I guess. Doesn't the princess like dogs?"

"It's not that. He picks up on people's anxiety, and I expect Princess Alice is stressed, so it won't do him any good to be around her."

Meatball wagged his tail.

"He's no trouble." And he'd be a perfect distraction while I talked to Alice.

"Leave him with me." The police officer petted Meatball on the head, while I stepped into the room.

I'd only been inside a few seconds, when a pillow was thrown at my head.

I almost lost the contents of the tray as I dodged to one side to avoid being hit. "Alice! It's me."

"Oh! Holly! I thought it was one of those awful policemen come to question me, or the doctor again." She launched herself off the bed and raced over to me. Her eyes were red-rimmed and her blonde hair a tangled mess around her head. "Everything is so awful."

"I know." I put the tray down and hugged her. "Everything will be fine. We're all working on a way to get this sorted."

She clung to me so tight, I almost couldn't breathe. "Everything's gone wrong. That nice lady is dead, your gran and Ray's wedding was ruined, Campbell is in trouble, and everyone thinks I'm a crazy killer."

I eased back from her grip. "I don't. I know you're innocent, and so does Campbell. Lots of people do."

She sniffed, her eyes watery. "My parents don't. They think I did it. They're doing a deal with the police to get me off on a technicality."

"I know all about that, and I don't agree with them," I said.

"I feel sick with worry. The doctor's talking about me going away for a long time and having some sort of re-education program. I don't think he's talking about how to learn advanced watercolors. Every time I ask questions, he gets this patronizing look on his face and tells me not to worry. And he's given me so many pills, I don't know which one to take when. I have pills to calm me down, pills to help me sleep, pills to wake me up. So many pills that I'd rattle if I took them all."

"Are you taking them?"

Alice shook her head. "Only when he insists. He says I need to relax, and even sedated me a couple of times, which I hate. I just want this to be over." Her gaze went to the tray. "What have you brought me?"

"Something to make you smile, I hope. Let's sit down and we can talk about this, but I don't have long. The police officer will think it's strange if I stay many minutes. I've left Meatball outside to distract him with his never ending cuteness."

"I don't want you leaving this room ever again. You have to stay with me," Alice said.

"I can't. As much as I want to, it'll look suspicious. We need to get down to business fast."

"Is it the officer with the long nose and the blue eyes?" Alice said.

"That's the one. What's he like?"

"He's not bad. Although not all that chatty." Alice lifted the lid off one of the cakes. "Oh, my favorite. Just what I needed. But we can use these for something more than soothing my battered heart." She lifted a plate off the tray and headed to the door before opening it. "Hello Mr. Police Officer, you must be bored out here. How about a cake to cheer you up?"

"That's kind of you, Princess, but I shouldn't while I'm on duty," he said.

"I've got too many. My assistant's been far too generous, and I need to watch my figure. Go on, I won't tell anyone." She held out the plate.

"It does look delicious, and I am hungry," he said.

"You take it. I can always get more. And you deserve it, you've been working so hard. I insist."

"Thanks. It looks great."

Alice closed the door and then turned to me, a smile on her face. "That'll keep him busy. Okay, what do we have to do?"

We settled on the bed with the rest of the cake and hot chocolate.

"I need you to think hard about the night of Daphne's murder. Any little detail could help prove your innocence."

Alice jutted out her bottom lip. "I've already told you this, and I told the police several times. I went up the stairs but don't remember much else."

"Why did you go up the stairs?"

Alice took a bite of the strawberry meringue and then held it out to me.

I shook my head. I was too anxious to eat.

"I was following your gran. I had a gift for her. It was special, and I wanted to give it to her when she wasn't busy."

"You followed my gran?"

"That's right. I had the gift in my room and thought it would be the perfect opportunity to give it to her when we were on our own. That's the last clear memory I have of that evening. Other than a few confusing flashes of action, I don't remember anything else."

"Let's go back a few steps. What were you doing before you went up the stairs?"

"Chatting to people, making new friends. I was having some of the delicious food at the reception. It was a really nice party."

"Did you speak to anyone in particular?"

"I was talking to the members of the band your gran booked. I congratulated them on how wonderful their playing was, and the singer was incredible. I was envious of her ability."

"Where were you when you were talking to them?"

"We were outside. They were taking a break from their set and having a few drinks. One of them, I think he played the guitar, was smoking a strange smelling cigarette. He offered it to me, but I don't smoke."

"That was most likely Jed," I said. "He mentioned he enjoyed the occasional herbal cigarette."

"Jed! That was his name."

"And it was after that you started feeling strange?"

Alice picked up the brownie. She took a bite, then pulled back and stared at it. "Yes! And I remember now. The singer gave me a brownie. She said it was a special brownie with a unique ingredient."

"You mean, Pearl? She's my gran's friend."

"That's right," Alice said. "I asked what was in the brownie, but she wouldn't tell me. It was a secret recipe. You know I love brownies, so I ate the whole thing, and it was delicious. Although not as delicious as this one."

"A special brownie?" I said.

"Yes. You don't think there was an ingredient in it that made me feel odd?" Alice said. "I don't have any allergies."

"Herbal cigarettes and special brownies," I said, more to myself than Alice.

"Pearl handed the brownies to everyone in the band and they all took some. If there was anything strange in them, it would have affected them all."

"Did Pearl eat a brownie?"

"I'm not certain. She probably did, although I didn't see. I was getting overheated, so decided to freshen up in the bathroom. That's when I saw your gran going upstairs. Everything gets fuzzy after that."

I gripped Alice's shoulders. "I think the brownie you ate had a drug in it. I don't know why Pearl gave it to you, but it sounds like she handed the drugged brownies to her band members, too."

"Oh! Did they also forget what happened that night?"

"They haven't said as much, but I should check. They could also have confused memories. And when I spoke to Pearl and Jed, they alibied for each other. What if Jed was going along with what Pearl said because he couldn't remember much about that night and didn't want to get in trouble? Especially since he was romancing Daphne in a closet not long before she died."

"I'm confused. Do you think Pearl killed Daphne? Why would she do that? And why drug me?"

Every muscle in my body tensed as I recalled what Gran said when I'd discovered her hiding in the apartment. She'd thought the killer had been after her. What if they'd made the same mistake as Alice and followed Daphne up the stairs thinking it was my gran?

Alice tugged on her arm. "Holly, what's going on? Have you figured something out? You've gone very pale."

"I'm ... not certain. Daphne had two injuries to her head. One on the back, and a big mark on her forehead. What if the killer also thought Daphne was my gran? Daphne was hit on the back of the head first. She could have turned around, and it was only then that the killer realized they'd hit the wrong person."

Alice gasped. "Just like I confused Daphne and your gran."

I was on my feet and moving to the door. What if I'd missed something? I needed to make sure Gran was safe.

"Are you certain about this? Who'd want your gran dead?" Alice followed me to the door.

"No, I'm not certain. I meant to ask Saracen to get one of his team to keep an eye on her, but it slipped my mind. I didn't think she was vulnerable." My hand shook as I clutched the door handle. "What if it was a case of mistaken identity? When Pearl realized she'd hit the wrong person, she had to finish Daphne off. Otherwise, she'd have told the police and Gran."

"If that's true, then your gran is in danger," Alice said.

I nodded. "I've got to go."

"Of course. Don't worry about me, I'll be fine. Nothing's happening to me until tomorrow. Go make sure your gran's okay. I'd feel terrible if anything happened to her because you were looking after me." Alice pulled me in for a tight hug again.

"Thanks, Alice." She felt more like a sister than a friend as I clung to her, needing her support as much as she needed mine. I wanted to be wrong about this, but my gut told me I wasn't. There were still pieces of this puzzle I was missing, but Gran was in danger, and I was terrified I'd be too late to save her.

Chapter 21

I burst out of Alice's bedroom, almost barging the police officer over.

"Hey! Is everything okay?" he said.

"No, nothing is okay." I headed down the stairs two at a time, Meatball at my heels. I had to get to Gran. I was an idiot. I'd been so focused on Reggie as the killer that I'd ignored the possibility Gran's life was at risk, even though she'd suggested it.

I pulled out my phone as I sprinted back to the apartment. "Saracen, it's my gran. She's in trouble. I need you to get to my apartment as quickly as you can."

"What happened to her?"

"I think the killer is after her."

"Reggie wants your gran dead?"

"It's not Reggie. It's Pearl. Hurry!" I shoved my phone back in my pocket, my lungs burning as I pumped my arms. I really hoped I was wrong about this. I'd be lost without Gran in my life. She hadn't been around for a long time, but I was used to her being here. She made my life so much brighter. Family was the most important thing, and I wasn't letting anything bad happen to mine.

Just as I reached the door of the apartment, pounding footsteps behind me made me turn. I let out a whoosh of air as I spotted Saracen bolting toward me.

"What's going on?" he said.

I shook my head and pressed a finger to my lips, then eased open the apartment door and poked my head inside. My stomach dropped to my feet and ricocheted back to my throat. Chairs were overturned, crockery was smashed on the kitchen floor, and the kitchen table was barged aside.

I hurried in. "Gran, are you here? It's Holly."

"Be careful," Saracen said as he looked at the chaos. "Whoever did this could still be inside. Let me go first."

I bounced from foot to foot as Saracen took the lead, his body coiled, ready to spring at the first sign of trouble.

We checked the lounge, which was empty, and then headed to the bedroom.

Saracen was about to open the door, when there was a scuffling on the other side.

"They're still here," he whispered to me.

"Gran could be hurt. Get the door open!"

Saracen eased open the door and flicked on the light. There was no one in the room.

"There's someone in here," Saracen said.

A scratching sound came from inside the wardrobe.

I raced over before Saracen could stop me and pulled open the door, expecting to see Gran tied up inside.

Saffron jumped out, her tiny body quivering, and her tail lowered.

"Oh! You poor little thing." I scooped her up.

Saffron whined and shivered as I held her.

"I wish you could talk," I said. "You'd tell me where Gran is. Was Pearl here? Did she attack Gran?"

"Why do you think your gran's friend is after her?" Saracen led the way out of the bedroom, and we did a quick check of the bathroom, and then looked out the back door into the yard, but there was still no sign of Gran.

"Alice remembered Pearl giving her a brownie just before her memory lapse. I think Pearl drugged Alice and her bandmates. And Gran mentioned this to me earlier, but I didn't take it seriously. She was worried that whoever killed Daphne was after her. They looked alike, especially from the back. But I couldn't see any reason why someone would want Gran dead, so dismissed it. But this mess looks like a fight happened, and now Gran is missing. Pearl also said she wanted to see Gran before she left. Was that so she could finish what she started?" I felt sick at the thought.

"Why does Pearl want your gran dead?"

"I have no idea. They're supposed to be friends. We have to find them." I pulled out my phone and dialed Gran's number. A phone rang in the lounge, and I hurried into the room, groaning when I spotted Gran's phone on the table.

"Let's look around outside," Saracen said.

"What if Gran's been hurt?" The words clogged in my throat.

"From what I know of your gran, she's a fighter. If Pearl is after her, she won't be easy to take down."

That did little to reassure me, but Saracen was right. I had to believe Gran was still okay.

Frustration filtered through me as the minutes ticked by and there was still no sign of Gran or Pearl outside. Every second, my panic grew.

A loud scream echoed from out of the woods, making me tense, then I was off and running in the direction it had come from.

"Holly, wait for me." Saracen was right behind me. "You don't know what you'll find."

"That was my gran! She's in trouble." I raced into the woods, Meatball tearing along beside me while I still held Saffron. "Find Gran, Meatball. Make sure she's safe."

Meatball led the way through the trees, his little legs a blur as he sped along. He loved Gran almost as much as I did.

"I hear voices up ahead," Saracen said. "Two women."

"That must be Pearl and Gran. Come on, we're close." My breath rasped out of me as I continued to run.

Meatball dodged around a bush and leaped over a fallen log. I followed him and almost lost my footing as my shoe caught on the tree trunk. Only Saracen's firm grip on my arm kept me upright.

There was a thud, followed by a yell.

"Just tell me where it is, and this will be over."

"That's Pearl," I said.

We stopped by the tree line, and I peered round a broad, gnarled oak tree. Gran and Pearl faced each other. Blood trickled down from Gran's hairline as she glared at Pearl.

Pearl held a large piece of broken tree branch in one hand, which she brandished like a weapon.

"You're out of your mind. I don't have any money," Gran said.

"You do. You always said you had a nest egg waiting for you when you got out of prison." Pearl lunged at Gran and whacked her on the shoulder with the tree branch.

Gran stumbled, almost falling to the ground, before turning and glaring at Pearl. "That was just talk."

"You said you'd made a fortune from fleecing rich older guys."

"I made some money before I got arrested," Gran said. "It was taken away from me. You don't get to keep the proceeds gotten through crime. I learned that the hard way."

"Liar! You hid some, I know it. You said you'd have enough to buy a house."

"Pearl, don't be stupid. I was bragging."

"Is your gran telling the truth about the money?" Saracen said.

"She is. And she's generous. If she has any-thing, she gives it away."

Pearl lunged at Gran again. This time, she got her around the waist and they fell to the ground, rolling over and tussling, curses flying from their lips like two drunken sailors in a bar brawl.

I rushed out of the tree line. "Hey, what's going on?"

Gran's head whipped around and her eyes widened. "Holly, get out of here. Pearl's lost her mind."

Pearl shrieked in Gran's face. "You're a greedy liar. We're supposed to be friends." She grabbed my gran's head and whacked it on the ground.

Saracen ran over and pulled Pearl off Gran. "Break it up, you two."

Pearl struggled in his grip. She kicked back, her foot slamming into Saracen's shin.

He grunted and dropped her on the ground.

Gran scrambled to her feet and backed away. Her clothes were dirty, and there was a streak of mud on her face mingled with the blood. "Leave, Holly. I can deal with Pearl. I've done it before. She's just forgotten her place in the pecking order."

"You don't have to fight," I said. "I heard she wants your money. Money you don't have."

"She has plenty of money." Pearl kept a wary eye on Saracen. "We always said when we got out, we'd look after each other. I need looking after, and she's not helping me."

"You don't need help. You make money from your singing gigs," Gran said.

"Not enough. We have big plans, and they don't come cheap."

"Is that what this has all been about?" I said. "You wanted money, so came after my gran?"

"I need a comfortable retirement," Pearl said. "I knew your gran was good for it."

"Your plan to get the money failed, though," I said.

"It was working fine until you and the beefcake showed up and interfered," Pearl said.

"We're not the problem. I meant, when you messed up by mistaking Daphne for Gran."

Gran's face paled. "So that's what happened. I always knew you hated me, Pearl."

"Of course, I did. You always got everything you wanted. Everyone liked you when we were inside, even the guards. You kept on bragging about all the money you had, and that you'd never need to work again."

Gran sighed and shook her head.

Pearl jabbed a finger at her. "We made an agreement, you, me, and Daphne. We'd watch out for each other. If ever any of us got in trouble, we'd help each other out."

"You don't need help," Gran said. "You're doing fine. You just got greedy."

"When did you realize you'd attacked the wrong person?" I said to Pearl.

She sucked in a breath. "I didn't hit Daphne. That was Princess Alice. And I hear she's about to be charged with murder."

"No, she's not," I said. "You drugged her and then tried to frame her. Did you pick her specifically, or was she in the wrong place at the wrong time?"

"That has nothing to do with me. I hear the princess has a screw loose," Pearl said. "Perhaps Daphne said the wrong thing to her, and she got angry."

"I don't believe Princess Alice had anything to do with what happened to Daphne. But I believe you did," Gran said. "You've always been spiteful. You hate it when someone has more than you, and you have to take it away. I saw you do it when we were in prison. You stole clothes, destroyed food, and even set a couple of people up because you didn't like them. I never thought you'd stoop so low as to go after Daphne."

"I didn't go after Daphne. I went after—" Pearl pressed her lips together.

"You went after my gran," I said. "And now we know why. But you wasted your time. Gran isn't wealthy."

Gran sighed. "I'm not, but I may have told the girls I was doing better than I was. You had to seem impressive to stay on top. I never thought it would come to this, though. My so-called friend turning on me for money."

Pearl dove at Gran, and she dodged out the way.

"Give up, Pearl," I said. "We've witnessed you attacking my gran, and we know the reason you wanted her dead."

"So what? That means nothing. It doesn't link me to what happened to Daphne," Pearl said, her fierce glare remaining on my gran. "You've got no evidence I had anything to do with that."

"Maybe a search of your things will turn up the drugs used on Princess Alice. We can also talk to your bandmates. Alice said you fed them brownies laced with the same drug. I expect their memories of that evening are hazy as well. And I bet they won't be pleased to learn you drugged them to make them more pliable to give yourself an alibi."

Two dots of color appeared on Pearl's cheeks. "My band will back me up. Unlike your gran, we're always there for each other."

"They won't back you up if they think you're a killer, because it could get them in trouble," I said. "And you are in trouble. You snuck after Daphne because you thought she was my gran. Did you hit her thinking you'd scare her, so she'd tell you where the money was hidden?"

"I ... I didn't do that."

"And when you realized your mistake, you had no choice but to kill her to keep her quiet. She cared for Gran and would have warned her you wanted her dead."

"Pearl, I'm ashamed of you," Gran said. "Daphne was a decent woman. She didn't deserve that."

"You never liked Daphne," Pearl sneered. "She used to drive you mad by always copying what you wore. You complained for days when she got her hair done in the same style as you. She was always trying to be like you.

She was a sad little loser. She's better off dead."

"You're a hateful woman for what you've done." Gran threw a punch at Pearl.

Pearl dodged back and aimed a kick at Gran's calf, then grabbed a rock off the ground and went to sling it at her.

Meatball barked and Saffron yipped. Then she leaped out of my arms, and the two dogs raced over to the fighting women.

Saffron grabbed Pearl's ankle and took a good, hard bite, while Meatball raced around her, snarling and issuing warning growls.

Pearl shrieked and dropped the rock she was about to hit Gran with. "Get it off me!"

Saracen marched over and caught hold of Pearl's arm. "I've heard enough. You're under arrest."

"Meatball!" I called him back with a pat on my leg.

Gran scooped Saffron away from Pearl's flailing limbs. "You're such a good girl for protecting me."

Saffron licked Gran's cheek and wagged her tail.

I raced over and hugged Gran. "I thought I was too late. I'm so sorry for not believing you."

She hugged me. "Don't be. After we talked, I convinced myself that my imagination was working overtime. It wasn't until Pearl appeared at the door and demanded money, that I realized I was right all along. I can't believe she killed Daphne."

I looked over at Saracen. "Are we all good?"

He nodded. "Great work, Holly."

I let out an exhausted sigh. "Come on, Gran. Let's get you home."

Chapter 22

It was the morning after Pearl had been caught fighting with Gran. I sat in the apartment, my gran and Ray at the kitchen table with me as we finished off a huge breakfast of maple syrup pancakes and a side order of strawberry scones.

Ray didn't drop his hold on Gran's hand the whole time they sat there, and he kept shooting her worried looks and asking if she was okay.

A knock at the door made me jump. I was still unwinding after yesterday's events. After all, discovering your gran was the target of a killer would shock anyone.

"Everyone relax," Gran said. "I doubt there's anyone else out there who wants me dead this week." She stood and walked to the door.

"That's not even the tiniest bit funny," I said. "I almost lost you yesterday."

"You didn't. Pearl got lucky when she hit me on the head. She only got in that one good shot. I was ready for her after that." Gran pulled open the door. "Alice! And Campbell. It's nice to see you both. Come in. I could do with a break from everyone being overprotective of me."

Alice hugged Gran. "We're all going to be protective of you. I've been hearing about the horrible things that happened. It's so awful. Ooh! Are those strawberry scones?" She hurried past my gran and to the table.

Ray stood and gave her his seat. "I'll make fresh coffee."

I looked over at Campbell, who stood stiffly by the door. "Get in here. Have a scone and a coffee and chill out."

He walked into the kitchen, seeming to fill the space with his broad frame, and nodded at me. "Thanks for getting this all sorted."

"I'm always happy to help right a wrong." I glanced at Alice. "Although I think you have a task to complete so you fulfill an obligation you have."

His gaze slid to Alice. "Not now."

I arched an eyebrow. "But soon. You said you'd do anything if I helped you."

He glared at me, grabbed the scone off my plate, and shoved it in his mouth.

There was another knock on the door, and Gran hurried to open it to reveal Saracen. "Come in, my knight in shining armor. Well, along with Holly, Saffron, and Meatball. It's only right you join in our celebratory break-fast."

Saracen grinned as he walked in. He nodded at Campbell. "I thought you'd all like to hear the news."

"Has Pearl been charged with Daphne's murder?" I said.

Saracen leaned against the kitchen worktop. "She spent all night denying it. Then Jed admitted he couldn't remember a thing about that evening after eating the brownie, and the drummer said he'd almost passed out. That was when she talked."

"What about the search of her things?" I said. "Did you turn up any memory suppressant drugs?"

"I'm getting to that," Saracen said. "We found the remains of the brownies in Pearl's things and ordered a rush job on the analysis."

"And ..." I held my breath.

"They contained drugs that would have messed with memory. After we revealed our findings to Pearl, she started talking about a deal, then confessed to everything when traces of the drugs were found in Princess Alice's blood sample."

"Those brownies were delicious," Alice said. "I'd never have known they contained drugs."

"You were lucky nothing serious happened to you," Saracen said. "The doctor confirmed there were two drugs used. A strong strain of cannabis, and a type of beta-blocker Pearl uses to help with her heart problems. Too much of that can cause permanent memory damage."

"That'll teach me to be greedy," Alice said.

"Pearl has heart problems?" Gran said.

Saracen nodded. "And it doesn't sound too good for her. She said she wanted the money from you to go out with a bang. She was planning a few long vacations and maybe a cruise before she got too ill."

Gran lowered her mug. "I don't like the thought of her being sick."

"That's no excuse for trying to kill you," I said.

Gran's lips thinned. "You're right. Maybe I'll send her a care package she can use in prison, though."

"I'm still at a loss to understand why Pearl drugged me? She drugged her bandmates to use them as her alibi. But where do I fit in?" Alice said.

"Don't take this personally, Princess Alice," Saracen said, "but Pearl suggested you were an easy target. She hadn't planned on framing anyone, but when you were talking to her at the wedding, Pearl realized how simple it would be to drug you and get you upstairs. And she said you talked about food a lot, so she knew you wouldn't turn down her brownie. She also figured if there was an obvious suspect found at the crime scene, there'd be less heat on her."

"Pearl thought I was a greedy idiot?" Alice's bottom lip jutted out.

"You're neither of those things," Campbell said. "You were just unlucky. She exploited you and that was wrong."

Alice fluttered her eyelashes at him and smiled. "I have you back to protect me from danger now."

"Pearl's always been cruel, Princess Alice. I often saw her mistreat new inmates. She'd act like their best friend, rob them blind, use them for whatever she could get, and then discard them. She enjoyed making other people unhappy."

"Why were you friends with her if she was so awful?" I said.

"It was a case of better the devil you know. I'd rather have had Pearl as a friend than an enemy when I was in there. And we continued to rub along when we got out. I never knew she was secretly after my money, and I can't believe she'd kill for it."

"Pearl's not going to hurt anyone else," Saracen said. "And it won't be a low security prison she ends up in this time. She's in the big leagues now, and she'll have tougher cellmates to deal with."

Gran shook her head. "It's such a shame. I've lost both my old friends."

Ray gave her a hug. "You've still got me."

"And me," Alice said.

"And me," I said. "We're not going anywhere."

Gran patted Ray's cheek and smiled at me. "Of course. My family is the most important thing."

Saffron whined and stood up against Gran's leg until she bent and picked her up.

"You, too. You're also my family." She kissed Saffron's head.

I looked over at Campbell. "There's something I'm confused about."

"You, confused? Usually, you have an answer for everything," Campbell said.

"You got suspended by the Duchess and arrested for kidnapping. How come you're here?"

"You can thank me for that," Alice said. "I've rehired him as my personal bodyguard. And after Pearl was taken in, I told the truth. Campbell had whisked me away for a secret date. He covered for me by saying he took me against my will to preserve my modesty."

I couldn't help the burst of laughter that shot out of me. "A secret date! Personal bodyguard! The police believed that?"

"Not all of it. I believe Peterson has been talking to the police commissioner. They're golfing buddies, so he's smoothing things over."

I shook my head. There were advantages to moving in well-connected circles. "And what does a personal bodyguard involve?"

Alice's cheeks flushed bright pink. "I need someone by my side while I go travelling in Europe for six months."

My joy faded. "You're going away?"

"I need a long vacation after this excitement." Alice grabbed my hand. "You must come with us. We can go wherever you like. Paris, Tuscany, Madrid. I've seen Europe loads of times, but it'll be an adventure for you."

I glanced at Campbell, only just managing to hold in my laugh at the angry expression on his face. "You two would be better off without me. You should see the sites together. You don't want me tagging along and getting in the way."

"You'd never be in the way," Alice said. "Are you sure you won't come with us?"

There was another knock at the door.

"Oh, my goodness. Who's that now?" Gran opened the door to reveal Rupert. "Lord Rupert, what a surprise. I expect you're here to see Holly."

He stepped inside and presented Gran with a huge bouquet. "I am, but these are for you. After your ordeal, you deserve a treat."

"You're such a sweet man." She kissed him on the cheek. "Don't I always say, Holly, Lord Rupert is so charming?"

"Only once or twice, Gran." I smiled at Rupert. I had my own reason for staying behind and not jet setting off with Alice, and he was standing in front of me, looking cute and slightly rumpled, as always.

"I've got a brilliant idea," Alice said. "The four of us should go away together. Me, Campbell, Rupert, and Holly. We'd have so much fun."

Campbell exchanged a glance with Rupert. Neither of them looked happy about that plan.

"We can talk about it another time," I said. "Right now, I want to enjoy the rest of my breakfast with my family and friends."

More coffee was poured and fresh scones removed from the oven, as everyone talked and laughed with each other.

I sat back and looked at my weird, wonderful, mixed up set of friends and family. Somehow, it all worked out perfectly.

Campbell glanced out the window as he drained his coffee mug. "Lord and Lady Audley are outside."

I tensed in my seat. I hadn't seen them since our last awkward encounter, but I couldn't keep ignoring them.

Alice jumped up and kissed Campbell on the cheek. "We must tell them about our vacation. We can meet up with them when we're out there. I'm sure we can make that happen. And they can't be mean to you, since they have a lot of making up to do after the way they treated me."

A panicked look entered Campbell's eyes. "Maybe we should stay away from your parents."

Rupert caught hold of my hand. "They do want to see you before they go. I told them they could come here before they left. I hope that's okay."

I gripped his hand. "It is. Since they will be my in-laws, I'd better mend some bridges with them."

"Yes, that's right. They ... hold on, did you just say they're going to be your in-laws?"

I grinned up at him. "That's right. If you still want me, I'd love to marry you."

Rupert swayed back and forth for a second before scooping me into his arms and giving me a big kiss on the lips. "I've been waiting for you to accept my marriage proposal for months. Yes! I absolutely want you to be my wife."

"What's this?" Alice raced over. "Have you accepted Rupert's proposal?"

I laughed as I stepped back from Rupert, feeling overwhelmed and excited by what I'd just agreed to. "It looks like it."

Alice flung her arms around me. "That's the best news in the world. Even better than when Campbell agreed to come away with me."

I caught Campbell's eye and shrugged. He rolled his eyes, but there was a smile on his face.

I extracted myself from Alice's arms. "Give me a minute before we celebrate. I need to clear the air with your parents."

"Oh, don't worry about them. They'll agree to anything. They're feeling so guilty after they tried to lock me up for being insane, I expect they'll even agree to me marrying Campbell."

"Alice! We should talk about that before you make plans," Campbell said, a pained look on his face.

She waved a hand at him. "And they'll have to buy me a stupidly big present. Maybe I can ask for a castle, or a horse. But then I'd have to take riding lessons again. They could pay for our trip around Europe. I'll think of something. Go on, Holly. What are you waiting for?" She shooed me away with her hands.

I caught hold of Rupert's elbow, and we headed to the waiting limo that sat in front of the apartment.

Lady Audley got out, her posture upright as she nodded at me. "We're leaving. It's been quite an adventure since we've been here."

"It's not always like this," Rupert said.

"Although it does have its moments," I said cautiously.

"So it would appear," Lady Audley said. "Miss Holmes, we would like to thank you for clearing our daughter's name. We were concerned she'd gotten herself in a muddle and wanted to put things right. It appears we didn't go about it in the most appropriate fashion. Alice spent some time telling us this last night after that terrible woman was caught."

"I never had any doubts about Alice," I said. "You have a wonderful daughter, and I consider her my best friend. She's sweet, generous, and funny. She's an asset to you. As is

Rupert." I sucked in a deep breath. "And we wanted you to be one of the first to know that I've accepted his marriage proposal. I will be joining your family."

Lady Audley's nostrils flared a fraction. "I think you'll make a good fit into our family. Make sure to give us plenty of notice when the wedding is, so we don't double book ourselves. We'll look forward to attending." She gave Rupert a rather formal kiss before simply nodding at me and sliding back into the limo.

I stood with Rupert as the car rumbled away.

"That went better than I expected," Rupert said. "They really must feel bad about what they tried to do to Alice."

"So they should."

He chuckled. "You should have heard her last night. Alice was amazing. She stood up to them about the whole murder business and then went on to list a dozen things she was unhappy about. She even told them she wasn't getting married to anyone they picked for her. She'd found someone she loved and was going to spend time with him."

"She told them about Campbell?"

"His name wasn't mentioned, but it's not hard to figure out who she was talking about." Rupert glanced over his shoulder. "And when Alice wants something, she always gets it, and then never lets go."

"Which is why I'm so glad we're friends. Life would be boring without you and Alice in it."

"Rupert! Holly, get back in here," Alice called from the doorway. "Your gran is making a batch of chocolate chip pancakes, and I want to hear all about the fight in the woods again. It sounds thrilling. I wish you'd taken pictures."

"My sister, she's so weird." Rupert led me back to the apartment.

I kissed him on the cheek. "We're all weird, and I wouldn't have it any other way. It's what makes us so perfect for each other."

I kissed him on the cheek. "We're all weird, and I wouldn't have it any other way. It's what makes us so perfect for each other."

Epilogue
Six months later

"You're twitching like you have ants in your pants. They'll be here." Gran stood in front of me as she teased the veil around my head.

"They can't be late, not today. Campbell is giving me away." I looked over my gran's shoulder along the gravel driveway leading away from Audley Castle. "I'm supposed to be walking up the aisle in ten minutes."

Meatball raced into the entrance, his black bow tie wonky. He presented me with a stick before running out again.

"Has Campbell ever let you down?" Gran stepped back. She wore a stunning jade green dress and a huge hat in the same color.

"Well, he's had his moments."

"That was before he realized what an asset you were. And what about Princess Alice? Do you think your best friend would miss your wedding? Especially since you're getting married to her brother."

"Alice would move heaven and earth to be here, but sometimes flights get delayed, or there's traffic. They can't control everything."

"And she'd have contacted you if that was the case. You focus on your big day." A smile crossed Gran's face. "My favorite granddaughter, finally marrying the man of her dreams."

"I'm your only granddaughter," I said.

She smoothed a curl off my cheek. "If I had a hundred granddaughters, you'd still be my favorite. And while I was inside, I met more of your extended family. Those Mistelthorpes are so posh, I keep resisting the urge to curtsy every time I meet one."

"You like them, though?"

"I do. I think they're charming."

My newly discovered family was here to see me get married to Rupert, along with the castle's kitchen staff, my stepmother, and stepsister. Plus, most of Rupert's family had turned out, so we had almost two hundred and fifty people at our wedding. Just thinking about that huge number watching me get married made me sweat.

My phone rang, and I looked at the caller display. "It's a work call. I should take it."

"Don't you dare. You're officially not working for the next three weeks."

I hesitated, not wanting to let down a customer. Ever since I'd accepted Rupert's marriage proposal, I'd taken a step back from my role in the kitchen, but I wasn't taking it easy. I now ran a small artistry baking business out of the castle. It was early days, but people loved my cakes and the orders were flooding in.

"Let me." Gran answered the phone. "This is Holly Holmes' assistant. Holly is getting married today, so she won't be doing any baking."

"But I will soon," I said. "Tell them to leave a message with what they want and I'll get back to them."

Gran simply arched an eyebrow. "Of course, I'll tell her that. Thanks for calling."

"What did they say? Is it the order for the cakes for the twenty-fifth wedding anniversary? I've got so many ideas."

"Stop thinking about cake. They wished you congratulations and look forward to working with you in the near future. Now, no more worrying about your business. It'll still be here when you get back from your honeymoon. Everyone will always want to eat your cakes, they just have to wait a bit longer than usual to get their sweet fix."

Someone cleared their throat behind me, and I turned to see Chef Heston dressed in a smart navy suit.

I hurried over, holding up the hem of my ivory dress. "Is everything okay with my wedding cake?"

He pursed his lips. "Of course it is. I made it."

"I tried to get in the kitchen last night to see if anything needed doing, but the doors were locked. I knocked for ages, but no one came."

"That was deliberate," he said. "We know what you're like when it comes to your cakes. We had to make sure you didn't spoil everything for your special day by interfering."

"It's my wedding cake! Surely, I should have been allowed to look."

"And you will, when it's brought out at the appropriate time during your reception. You'd have only messed with the decorations if you'd seen it."

I sighed. It had caused me physical pain not to bake my own cake, but Chef Heston insisted it was his wedding gift to me, so I could hardly refuse.

"Did you add the red velvet layer?" Gran walked over.

"I did," Chef Heston said, with a nod to Gran.

"And the lemon?"

"As requested."

"I hope you didn't forget the chocolate."

"Gran! How big is this cake?"

She chuckled. "Huge! We have a lot of mouths to feed."

"The cake is perfection." Chef Heston held out a small silver box. "This is for you, from all of us in the kitchen."

"A gift?" I stared at the box. "What is it?"

"Open it and take a look."

I lifted the lid and gasped. Inside was a beautiful silver charm bracelet. On it was a tiny cupcake charm, a spoon, and a baking bowl.

"It's stunning," Gran said.

"We all wanted you to have something to remember us by. And those charms seemed appropriate," Chef Heston said.

Tears filled my eyes, and I quickly blinked them away. "It's perfect. I'm not going anywhere, though. I still want to come in the kitchen and see how everyone is doing."

"Maybe I won't let you in, since you no longer work for me." Chef Heston lifted his brow.

"Oh! I mean, I understand if you don't, but you're always welcome to any of the recipes I create. I ... I'll miss the kitchen."

"I may let you in, so long as you don't distract the team. And customers are already asking if there'll be a special display case with the fancy cakes in." He snorted, then smiled. "As if my cakes aren't fancy enough. But we'll be placing plenty of orders with you soon."

"Not until after the honeymoon," Gran said.

Chef Heston nodded. "Of course. Have a wonderful wedding, Holly. I should go inside and find a seat."

I kissed his cheek. "Thanks, Chef Heston. For everything."

"It's always been entertaining working with you, Holly. Enjoy your day." He turned and walked into the castle.

"Gran, help me put this bracelet on." I held out my wrist.

She fastened the charm bracelet for me. "Even though he's as grumpy as they come, I don't mind that Chef Heston."

"He was a great boss, even though he yelled at me too much." I looked out the door again. "Any sign of Alice and Campbell?"

Meatball ran in and barked. He trotted back to the entrance and wagged his tail.

"I'd say that's a yes," Gran said.

My heart pounded as I spotted a car speeding toward us. "They made it!"

"I knew they wouldn't let you down." Gran kissed my cheek. "I'd better get inside, too. You look so beautiful, Holly. I'm proud of you." She gave me another kiss and then headed through the doors.

A few seconds later, the car skidded to a halt. Alice tumbled out of the passenger door, a lipstick in her hand. "I'm so sorry. We had everything planned, and then we got stuck in traffic, my phone battery died, then Campbell said he knew a shortcut, but he got lost, and—"

"I didn't get lost, but one of the roads was closed." Campbell strode around the side of the car. He was dressed in a black tuxedo, his chin cleanly shaven, looking a bit like a scary version of James Bond. He gripped Alice's shoulders. "Take a few deep breaths. We made it."

"I'm just glad you got here," I said. "I didn't want to walk that aisle on my own."

Meatball barked and lifted one paw.

I grinned down at him. "Of course, you'd have been with me."

Alice smoothed down her pale amber bridesmaid's dress and then hugged me. "We shouldn't have left it 'til the last minute, but I wanted to show Campbell the caves in Tuscany, and we couldn't get an earlier slot. I was so certain it wouldn't be a problem." Her face lit up as she smiled at me. "Don't you look lovely. Doesn't Holly look beautiful, Campbell?"

"You look very nice, Holmes," Campbell said.

"Thanks. So do you. Everyone is here. And I mean, everyone. Even your parents made it," I said to Alice.

"Don't worry about them causing trouble. They've been on their best behavior for months. You just focus on my brother. I bet he's grinning like an idiot waiting for you."

"We shouldn't keep him waiting any longer," Campbell said. "Are you ready, Holly?"

"As ready as I'll ... Hey, what's that on your ring finger?" I pointed to the enormous sparkling rock on Alice's left hand.

She sucked in a breath and hid her hand behind her back. "I meant to take it off before we got here. I don't want to outshine your special day."

I stared at Campbell. "Have you asked Alice to marry you?"

He lifted one shoulder. "We decided it was the right thing to do."

"You shouldn't have hidden this from me. I'm thrilled for you both."

"I'm so glad you said that," Alice said. "I've been bursting to tell you, but Campbell said it wasn't the right time. This is all about you and Rupert, and I don't want to take the limelight away from you."

"I don't mind not being the center of attention." I grinned at Alice. She was glowing with happiness, and even Campbell looked softer around the edges, a smile on his face as he looked at Alice.

"You must be my bridesmaid when it's my turn," Alice said. "And I'm having a unicorn theme. I can't believe you turned down that idea. It was genius."

"I'm not sold on the unicorns," Campbell said.

"Unicorns are a bit over the top for me, too. I was trying for a small, understated wedding," I said.

"There's nothing understated about having the entire Audley family come to your big day," Campbell said. "And I hear the Mistelthorpes have also turned out."

"How do you know that?" I said.

"I might not work here anymore, but I have inside contacts."

I grinned. "Saracen's been doing an amazing job since you've been away. He's handled everything. He'll need a vacation when all this is over."

Gran poked her head out the door. "Everyone's getting restless. What's the hold-up?"

Alice slipped the engagement ring off her finger and placed it in her purse. "Nothing. We'll be right there. Holly's just having a wobble."

"I'm not! I can't wait to marry Rupert." I had zero doubts that this change would be amazing. I was looking forward to spending the rest of my life being blissfully happy with my new husband, baking cakes, and hopefully not getting tangled up in any more murders. Well, maybe a little crime solving on the side would be fun.

"And so you shall. Come on, let's get you married." Alice hugged me again. She settled in position in front of me, ready to walk in on the waiting wedding party, then turned and gave me a thumbs up, just before the main door opened.

"Are you ready for your next big adventure, Holmes?" Campbell tucked my hand through his elbow and winked at me.

A jumble of excitement and joy swirled through me and I nodded. "I've never been more ready for anything in my whole life."

About Author

K.E. O'Connor (Karen) is a mystery author living in the beautiful British countryside. She loves mystery, animals, and cake.

When she's not writing, she volunteers at a local animal sanctuary, reads a ton of books, binge watches mystery series, and dreams about living somewhere warm.

Stay in touch! (and receive an exclusive **FREE** Holly Holmes novella.)

Website: www.keoconnor.com/freebooks

Facebook: www.facebook.com/keoconnorauthor

Complete series list

Enjoy the Holly Holmes culinary mysteries in large print, paperback, and e-book.

Cookie Crumble and Murder

Cream Caramel and Murder

Chocolate Swirls and Murder

Vanilla Whip and Murder

Cherry Cream and Murder

Blueberry Blast and Murder

Mocha Cream and Murder

Lemon Drizzle and Murder

Maple Glaze and Murder

Mint Frosting and Murder

I hope you enjoyed this fun culinary mystery. It was a delight to write.

I have a special treat for you. Here's a delicious recipe with a maple theme!

Enjoy these maple cookies. Granny Molly approved.

Recipe
Canadian Maple Cookies

Prep time: 15 minutes   **Cook time**: 10 minutes

MAKES 30

Recipe can be made dairy and egg-free. Substitute milk for a plant/nut alternative, use dairy-free spread, and mix 3 tbsp flaxseed with 1 tbsp water to create one flax 'egg' as a binding agent (this recipe requires 3 tbsp flaxseed to substitute 1 egg.)

INGREDIENTS

1/2 cup (100g) unsalted butter, softened

1/2 cup (100g) brown sugar, packed

1 small egg

1/2 cup real maple syrup

1 teaspoon vanilla extract

2 cups (300g) all-purpose flour

1 teaspoon baking soda

⅓ cup (70g) granulated sugar

INSTRUCTIONS

1. Preheat oven to 350F (175C)

2. Grease 2 cookie sheets or use non-stick baking paper.

3. Cream butter and brown sugar.

4. Add the egg, maple syrup, and vanilla, mixing until blended.

5. Mix flour and baking soda. Add to the creamed mixture and stir.

6. Shape into 1 inch balls and roll in the sugar.

7. Place balls on cookie sheets about 2 inches apart and flatten.

8. Bake for 8-10 minutes.

9. Remove and let cool on a wire rack.

10. Enjoy!

If you enjoyed Maple Glaze and Murder, keep reading for an extract from a festive Christmas special: **MINT FROSTING AND MURDER!**

Chapter 1

"I only managed two verses of Silent Night before a string broke on my harp. The carol ended up sounding more like Blue Christmas once I'd mangled my way through it. I should have stopped, but I was so looking forward to playing at the church service." Princess Alice Audley leaned on the kitchen counter as I stored leftover cakes in the Audley Castle industrial fridges.

And we had a surprising number of sweet treats left over. There was nothing wrong with the festive frosted donuts, cinnamon crisp apple tarts, or iced yule log, but the freezing weather meant visitors weren't brave enough to leave their homes, even for a slice of delicious cake and a wander around the festively decorated castle.

"You said learning to play the harp wasn't your thing. See the broken string as a sign," I said.

"A sign I'm useless at learning anything." Alice poked her bottom lip out.

"You're excellent at plenty of things."

She arched a pale blonde eyebrow. "Name them. I don't expect the list will be long."

I placed the final tray of gingerbread iced cookies in the chiller cabinet. "You're kind, generous, you always make me laugh, you're thoughtful, and—"

"That's my character. What about the things I'm good at? You're an excellent baker and great at historical research. What do I excel in? Making a harp sound like I've trodden on a cat's tail?"

"You could be good at anything you put your mind to." I adored my best friend, and sister-in-law, but her wonderfully blonde ditzy head got turned too easily when she found the latest thing to learn. It meant she didn't stick at much for long. Although we stuck to each other, and that was good enough for me.

Alice flipped her hair over one shoulder. "When I spoke to Paris on the phone today, she reminded me one of our tutors said I only had half a brain, and if it weren't for my family legacy, I'd be a nothing."

"That tutor should have been fired." I turned to face Alice. "I hope your friends stuck up for you."

"Not really. If anyone spoke out in that class, they got picked on next. Everyone says going to a posh school provides you with the best education, but I wonder. I'd have been better going to a poor school like you. You didn't turn into too much of a delinquent."

"Princess Alice Audley! Don't be a snob. Maybe my school didn't have antique wooden desks, feather quills, and tutors wandering around in long robes, but I got a decent education."

She giggled. "You're describing Hogwarts."

I grinned at her. "I always get an image of that place when you talk about the colleges your parents sent you to."

"Hmmm... I don't know. I don't feel like I learned much. Certainly nothing useful. What's the point of Latin these days? Or knowing how low to curtsy when meeting someone with a particular noble title? You got everything you needed to have a successful career."

"I'm not sure being complained at by Chef Heston every day is everyone's perfect career path." Even though my boss could be a red-faced, shouting pain in my behind, I wouldn't change a thing about my job in the

Audley Castle kitchen. It was stressful, the customers were demanding, but I adored baking. Almost as much as I adored my perfect little dog, Meatball.

"It's not every day, now." Alice smoothed a hand down her red gown. She'd been wearing festive colors since the beginning of December. Sometimes, she added tinsel around her neck. "Not since you've gone down to working part time. You're practically a lady of leisure since you married my brother."

I swatted Alice's hand away from the mint frosted cupcakes we'd been perfecting. "I still work four days a week. But now I'm with Rupert, it's nice to spend more time together." I smiled to myself. I'd been married to Lord Rupert Audley for almost eighteen months. After plenty of road bumps and diversions, we'd plucked up the courage to admit our feelings for each other.

And Rupert was exactly the kind of husband I knew he would be. Loyal, loving, funny, still with his nose permanently in a book, wonderfully clumsy, and always there when I needed him.

Alice's sigh swerved toward the dramatic. "I hate seeing you two together."

"Why?"

"Because you remind me of everything I don't have with Campbell."

"Alice, you and Campbell are great together. Although I never thought I'd see it happen. The man keeps his emotions so tightly buttoned up, I wondered if he was an android before he declared his feelings to you."

Alice and Campbell Milligan, the head of Audley Castle security, had dated for as long as Rupert and I were married. Alice had always had a huge crush on the surly, uptight, occasionally clever man, and he'd always been hopelessly in love with her. He'd just never admitted it.

She giggled again. "It does take work to get him to admit how he's feeling. His default answer when I ask him is always 'fine.' But he's been so grumpy since his accident. He's even trying my patience, and I've been in love with him for years."

"Last time I spoke to him, he reminded me of a hungry grizzly bear." Campbell had broken his foot and was covered in bruises after his brakes failed and he flipped a car into a ditch. Fortunately, he'd been the only one in the vehicle, but everyone had been worried about him. Alice had fainted when she'd heard he'd been in an accident, and when she'd come to, had been convinced he wouldn't pull through.

Unsurprisingly, Campbell made an awful patient. He hated being sick and told me he didn't have time to be unwell. But he had no choice but to submit to bedrest, since a broken foot took weeks to heal, and he wasn't allowed to put any weight on it. Doctor's orders.

"I'll take some cakes up to him after we've finished," Alice said. "Even though he never likes to admit it, your baking cheers him up."

"I've noticed him indulge a time or two in the past. Although I've also heard him complain you're feeding him too much and he'll get fat."

"Impossible! That man is all muscle." Alice sighed. "As much as I'd love to drool over his delicious muscles—"

"Please, don't."

She tutted. "We must focus on these cakes. I must ensure whatever we bake is spectacular, so I can impress my friends when they get here. I will perfect my chocolate cake."

I glanced out of the high windows. Snow had steadily fallen for two days. It hadn't let up once, and fifteen inches lay on the ground, making the castle frostily stunning in the lead up to Christmas. But being in the countryside in the beautiful village of Audley St. Mary meant the way in to the castle was tricky to navigate by car or foot.

"Are you sure they'll make it? Lots of people have already cancelled."

"They wouldn't dare miss Christmas at Audley Castle. We've been talking about it for months. Those ladies will find a way. And when they get here, everything has to be perfect."

I was already pulling out ingredients to make a fresh batch of mint chocolate frosted cupcakes with gingerbread men topping. "Your friends will love your baking, even if you don't think it's perfect. After all, you went to the effort of making it for them. They'll appreciate that."

She waggled a finger in my face. "Uh-uh. You've never met these particular friends, have you?"

"No, but I've heard plenty about them. They're your friends from boarding school, right?"

"Yes, we were in the same house. I wouldn't say we were natural friends, but when you get thrown together in a strange environment full of terrifying rules, bond quickly to survive."

"You make your boarding school sound like a prisoner of war camp."

"Sometimes, that's what it felt like. The tutors were mean. But I survived, and in part, it was thanks to my boarding school sisters. Because of that, we have an unbreakable bond." Alice wrinkled her adorable button nose. "They can be beastly when they want to, though. Which is why I'll show them my life is idyllic. And I'll prove that being voted most likely to say something stupid on a first date, and spend all my money on something dumb, was unfounded."

I paused from measuring out the cinnamon. It was a smell that reminded me of Christmas. "Did they really do that?"

"It was a joke. But I didn't find it funny." Alice grabbed my arm, causing me to fling flour in the air from the pack I held. "Make sure you don't mention I bought one hundred glittering wind chimes and put them around the castle. Those things drove Granny crazy."

"I suppose you don't want me to mention the money you invested in the doggy day spa, either?"

"That sounded like a sensible business investment. How was I to know dogs don't like saunas and hot tubs?"

"You could have asked Meatball." My delightful tan and white corgi cross was snoozing at home, no doubt in front of a roaring open fire after being spoiled by Rupert.

"Perhaps it wasn't the wisest investment." She grabbed a chocolate cupcake off the tray we'd already made. "Keep that just between us."

I grinned at her. Alice could have her head in the clouds, but she was smart and determined when she really wanted something. "We'll prove them wrong."

"I know we will. Because you're an amazing friend, and an even better sister-in-law." She wrapped me in a huge hug. "I couldn't have wished for a better one. Even though my daft brother took long enough to put a ring on your finger. I was worried he'd lose you to someone else."

Fortunately for me and Rupert, I'd had a crush on him since starting work at Audley Castle. I'd never thought it would come to anything, though. After all, he was a lord, and I was a commoner who worked in the castle kitchens. But true love shone through, and nothing could stop us from finding our way to each other. Even though the road was one of the windiest and most confusing I'd ever walked.

Chef Heston marched into the kitchen, still wearing his chef's whites. He slowed and stared down his long, thin nose at us.

"Princess Alice. I thought you'd be finished by now. Do you need more time in the kitchen?"

Alice beamed at him. "We're just getting started. I tried to make some Christmas cookie crumble with the sweet mincemeat Holly made." She pointed at a burned offering on the counter. "It's all my fault. Holly said to watch the timer, but I got distracted when making icing for the cupcakes. Before I knew it, smoke billowed out of the oven."

I held back a smile as Chef Heston gritted his teeth.

"These things happen." His gaze shifted along the counter. "May I ask what that is?"

A sunken fruitcake sat next to the burned sweet mincemeat cookie crumble.

"That was my third attempt at a traditional Christmas cake. We put brandy and whiskey in this one. And when Holly's back was turned, I added a couple of extra measures of alcohol. I wanted it to be extra delicious. Then it wouldn't firm up. The edges got overdone, but the middle stayed soggy." Alice's mouth twisted. "Maybe you need a new oven."

"If I may, Princess, the oven is fine. Perhaps you put too much liquid in the cake." Chef Heston glowered at me. "You must use exact measurements. A decent instructor would tell you that."

"Holly did! I thought I was making things better. Still, third time is a charm. We're making mint frosted chocolate cupcakes next. Well, again. They'll work this time. We just need to sprinkle them with Christmas magic."

"A word, Holly." Chef Heston caught hold of my elbow and escorted me out of the kitchen and into the corridor. "Please, make her stop."

"Baking? But Alice is having fun."

"I'm begging you. She's wasting supplies. Don't think I missed the two ruined trays of food outside. The bottoms of the cookies were black!"

"Um… that was supposed to be a gingerbread wreath and sugar cookies with Christmas frosting. Alice got—"

"Distracted. Yes, she does that. But the snow has closed most of the roads leading to the castle. Half the Christmas food I've ordered has yet to arrive, and I can't see it getting here in time. The Christmas Day feast will be a disaster."

"Maybe some deliveries won't make it, but there's enough food in the store to last us a month."

"Only basic supplies. The festive ham and the gold crown turkey haven't been delivered. And I arranged for an imported European figgy pudding for the Duke. He adores his figgy pudding."

"You make an amazing figgy pudding. All you need are eggs, sugar, breadcrumbs, spices, dried fruits, suet, and brandy. What you'll make will be better than the one you spent all that money on."

"Of course it will, but it won't be the same. The Duke will know. And he expects things to be done a certain way." Chef Heston wrung his hands together. "Christmas is such a special event at the castle, but this weather will ruin everything. Most of the party guests have canceled."

I'd never seen Chef Heston this stressed, and his stress level usually simmered at a red-faced eight on a good day. "It can still be special. This year, the snow may make things a little different."

"Not just the snow. Last Christmas, you were my kitchen assistant, not a member of the family. You won't get a moment's peace, you know. You'll be expected to attend one event after another, go to all the local gatherings, and be a voice for the castle. Everyone will want to talk to you."

I bit my bottom lip. I didn't mind the occasional social event, but I wasn't a woman who enjoyed back-to-back parties. I needed down time with my dog, a plate of cookies, and my feet up. "That does sound exhausting."

He grunted. "That's what you get for marrying into the Audleys. People expect things from you. You're a part of the village. An important part."

"I like to think I was always special, not just because I married Rupert."

I got another grunt for that comment. But I understood what Chef Heston meant, and I'd experienced my share of social events and expectations since getting married. It was another reason I'd reduced my working hours. The family were active village patrons, and involved with many charities. We were always getting invitations to opening events, ceremonies, and galas. I found it intimidating, but I loved being involved in a community that had warmly welcomed me when I'd moved to Audley St. Mary.

"We can handle this. We know our way around the kitchen, so we'll make Christmas perfect for everyone," I said.

Chef Heston did a mock curtsy. "Whatever you say, Lady Holly."

"Oh, no. When I'm in the kitchen, I'm plain old Holly to you."

"If that's true, then get back in there and clear up the mess Princess Alice has made. Keep an eye on her and make sure she stays out of my precious supplies. She's a disaster. I don't know why I put up with her?" A rare smile crossed his face.

For all Chef Heston's bluntness and occasional rudeness, he had a good heart and a passion for making delicious food. He also had a soft spot for Princess Alice.

There was an enormous crash as metal hit the stone floor in the kitchen, making us both jump.

"Go! Now! Stop her before she burns the place down."

"I'm on it." I hurried away and poked my head around the door into the kitchen.

Alice was scooping up baking trays. She looked up at me and there were tears in her eyes.

I dashed into the kitchen. "What's the matter?"

She dumped the trays on the counter and sniffed. "I wanted to make sure Campbell had the perfect Christmas. He's been so down since the car accident. I wanted to give him something to smile about."

"He'll have a great Christmas with you. He's just in pain and hates taking his medication.

He thinks it makes him look like less of an alpha male because he needs help."

"That would be impossible. My wonderful boyfriend is all alpha."

I resisted the urge to roll my eyes. I'd witnessed that alpha in action many times. He was as stubborn-headed as he was in love with Alice. "In a few weeks, the worst will be over. Campbell will be walking again, even if it is on crutches, then you can make plans for the New Year together."

"But I figured Christmas would be the perfect time to show him what a wonderful wife I could be."

My jaw dropped. "Wife! Is he thinking of proposing to you?"

"No. I'm planning on proposing to him."

Ready to indulge in some Mint Frosting and Murder? Available in large print, e-book, and paperback.